BET ON LOVE
KANI SEY

First Published in Great Britain in 2021 by
LOVE AFRICA PRESS
103 Reaver House, 12 East Street, Epsom KT17 1HX
www.loveafricapress.com

Text copyright © Kani Sey, 2021
All rights reserved.
No part of this publication may be reproduced, stored or transmitted in any form by any means, electronic, mechanical, photocopying or otherwise, without the prior permission of the publisher, except in the case of brief quotations embodied in reviews.
The right of Kani Sey to be identified as the author of this work has been asserted by them under the Copyright, Design and Patents Act, 1988
This is a work of fiction. Names, places, events and incidents are either the products of the author's imagination or used fictitiously. Any resemblance to actual persons, living or dead, is purely co-incidental.

---

1. http://www.loveafricapress.com

BLURB

Despised and constantly degraded, Binta can't wait to leave home when she discovers her family never wanted her. She is determined to cut a path and succeed in her life without love and emotional connections. Until she bumps into her former best friend, Bass.

Once upon a time, Bass was head-over-heels in love with Binta. But she shattered his heart, and he had to move on without her. A chance encounter with her five years later brings back all the buried emotions.

However, it seems Binta hasn't overcome her trust issues. This time, though, Bass is not willing to walk away so readily. Can he convince her to bet on their love?

ACKNOWLEDGEMENTS

I would like to extend my eternal gratitude to Awa Senghore, Musa Bah, Fatou Jeng, Talibeh Hydara, Hassan Hydara, Pa Modou Drammeh, Fatoumatta B. Bah and Yata Ndow.

Your unflinching support and motivation has always given me that extra push and inspiration a writer always needs.

For Fatoumatta Suwareh, my self-proclaimed number one fan. Thank you for always being that one reader I could count upon.

CHAPTER ONE

The steady drip of rainwater into the buckets matched Binta's rhythmic heartbeat.

She tossed and turned a couple of times on her lumpy mattress and finally rolled onto her back, staring at the cardboard ceiling that had more holes in it than a basketball hoop. All the buckets she'd placed on the floor overflowed.

Her teeth clattered with cold as the icy wind seeped into her bones. She tried to warm up by pulling the sheets over her head, but it was no use.

How could it be?

The wooden planks she'd used to patch up the broken windows clearly couldn't protect her from the weather's harsher elements.

Especially not during a thunderous raging storm, showing no sign of abating. October was always a wild month, full of powerful storms that wreaked a lot of havoc.

Her heart went out to those whose compounds were always affected during storms like these. During last year's rainy season, one of the homes in the neighbourhood collapsed. Some families would probably spend the whole night trying to keep the water at bay.

Her situation was bad enough, but it would end soon.

No longer would she have to sleep in this wretched draughty storeroom.

After tonight, she wouldn't have to live in this horrible house where everybody hated her.

Renting the new apartment was the right thing to do; she knew this with all her heart.

Thanks to the great job she'd gained after finishing her Bachelor's degree in Banking and Finance at the university, she'd be able to live on her own.

Her hard work and perseverance had begun to pay off, rewarding her with professional success.

The rain fell in torrents. Without warning, the part of the ceiling directly above the mattress cracked wide open. A cold blast of rain soaked Binta's skin before she could leap out of its way.

"Uh!" Shivering, she grabbed her towel from a stool and began to dry herself.

Couldn't the ceiling have waited until she had moved out? Where would she spend the rest of the night?

She could creep into Isatou's bedroom. The princess of the house would be fast asleep by now.

Making up her mind, she moved her damp mattress out of the way and placed a laundry pan in its place to prevent water from overrunning the room. She took out fresh bedsheets from her suitcase and headed for her younger sister's bedroom.

Careful not to make any sounds that could wake the other girl, Binta closed the bedroom door and walked into the carpeted room.

A crackle of lightning illuminated the room.

Isatou was fast asleep.

Binta knew better than to climb into the bed. She spread one of her sheets on the carpet and used the other to cover herself.

A yelling voice drifted into Binta's consciousness, accompanied by someone shaking her violently.

She opened her droopy eyes to a room full of blinding white light.

Isatou had switched on the bulb. She wore a brown wrapper and a sleeveless white blouse. Still, the expression on her face was utterly dark and accusatory. "What are you doing in my room? *Gaenal fi!*"

"Calm down, Isatou," Binta placated in a sleep roughened voice. "The rainwater is falling into my room, and my mattress is wet. Just let me sleep here for tonight."

"Binta, I don't care if the Atlantic Ocean has shifted to the storeroom. *Suma yoon nekusi,*" her sister shot back. "It is where you belong, and it is where you are going to sleep. Now get the hell out of my room!"

"Isatou, if you could—"

"Get out!" she screeched at the top of her lungs, the pounding rain wasn't loud enough to drown it out.

Binta's heart rate accelerated with fear as she heard the banging of their parents' bedroom door. They would be here any second now. She hastily got up from the floor as they entered the room.

"*Yaa, nyan nala*, tell her to get out of my room," Isatou whined to their mother, placing her head on Musu's shoulder.

"How dare you enter your sister's room and disrupt her sleep?" Musu bit out. "Have you lost your senses? Shouldn't you know better? Get back to the storeroom!"

"I can't, *Yaa*. The rain has—"

"Talking back at your mother now?" her father cut in. "I will give you a whooping you will never forget if you do not do as you are told right now."

Binta's heart filled with dread. "Just let me sleep in the sitting room then. You all know I'm moving out tomorrow."

"Oh, yes! Got yourself a fancy little apartment, didn't you?" Her mother taunted, placing hands on her hips. "You are finally going to get the freedom that will be your ruin. Only a young unmarried woman who wants to run around with men will live alone, *ningaa nyaka jom*! But since you are under our roof tonight, you'll sleep where we tell you to."

Her mother's words cut her deeper than she should have allowed them to. One would have thought she'd be used to these insults heaped on her daily.

"Will it kill you to treat me like a daughter for once?" she shouted out loud. Years of suffering in silence, bearing emotional and psychological abuse and she'd reached her breaking point. The dam holding all her emotions at bay burst wide open.

"What have I ever done to merit such hostility and hatred from my own parents? I've always respected and obeyed you at my own expense. I've always taken in all the hardships you put me through without a single complaint while I watched you treat Isatou like a princess. You've never cared about my well-being, *fall-*

eh wulen whether I eat or sleep or even live. I don't even think you would care if I died!"

"You ungrateful insolent chit!" her mother yelled. "We've fed, clothed, and put a roof over your head for twenty-four years. What more could we have possibly given you?"

"A child needs more than that from her parents," she whispered brokenly. The sneaking suspicion she had lived with coiled around her heart, compelling her to finally voice it out. "Or is it that you are not my real parents? Did you really give birth to me?"

"No, we are not your real parents," Babucarr replied without hesitation, his face full of scorn.

The world caved under Binta feet.

"What?" she breathed.

"You heard him. Your parents didn't want you, and we took you in out of pity," Musu spat out. "If we had known you would turn out like this, we would have left you in the wilderness to rot."

The thunderclap shooting through the sky seemed to be a confirmation of her despicable words.

Binta stared at the two people she had always thought were her parents, and the look on their faces told her everything she needed to know.

"It all makes sense now," Isatou derided as Binta began to walk out of the room in a ghostlike trance. "I always wondered how I could be related to someone like her."

Numb with heart-breaking shock, Binta returned to the storeroom and sat on top of her suitcase. Her body trembled from the cold, but she was oblivious to its effect. Pain sliced through her heart, blotting out everything else.

Isatou was right. It all made sense now.

Her birth parents didn't want her. Neither did the people who'd raised her.

She was the problem. What was wrong with her? What was so horrible about her that she couldn't be loved?

AS THE HAZY LIGHT OF dawn began to trickle from the sky, washing away the darkness of the night, the cobwebs in Binta's head began to clear.

A master at compartmentalising her feelings, she knew what she had to do.

She would lock all the dark emotions awakened from last night's revelations in the farthest corners of her mind.

The only way she could perform well at work.

Being the manager of a bank branch wasn't child's play, and she couldn't afford to put her job at risk as it was the only good thing she had in her life.

The position had come easy to her seeing as she'd graduated with honours, at the top of her class. Her impeccable credentials had more than made up for her lack of experience.

Taking a deep calming breath, she got up from her suitcase and made ready to go to work. After taking a shower and praying, she dressed in a knee-length chocolate-coloured cotton skirt, a matching jacket, and a crisp white blouse underneath. She combed her hair extension and tied it back in a ponytail. She slipped into her comfortable but classy block heel shoes and grabbed her black leather handbag.

She looked around the storeroom, sure that she never wanted to return.

Almost all her things were in the new apartment. Her friend, Maimuna, had already promised to move the remaining stuff while she was at work.

There was nothing left here for her, and the idea of a fresh start had never been so appealing.

SKY HIGH BANK WAS ONE of the most prosperous banks in the country with a wide variety of clientele and extensive branch offices.

Binta was the newly appointed manager of a branch located at the heart of one of the busiest metropolises in the urban area. Mayor Yankuba Colley Avenue was perhaps the most industrious in Serrekunda.

The businesses lining the avenue ranged from food, magazines to beauty product stores.

The Serrekunda branch of the Sky-High Bank stood between a foreign exchange bureau and a prestigious textile shop.

It was an attractive building painted in shades of sea green and yellow. Giant terracotta pots of flowers adorned the entrance.

Binta murmured a greeting to the security guard as he held the heavy glass door open for her. Her block heels resounded on the bank's tiled floor as she walked by the employees under her command. The tellers were setting up in their respective stations as the bank was about to be open to customers.

A smile of genuine pleasure crossed her lips. Stepping into her workplace always gave her a sense of belonging and purpose that was exhilarating.

This was a place where she was respected even if she wasn't liked. Some of the older staff didn't like having a younger woman in charge.

Still, it was a place where her skills and brilliance were needed and appreciated. People looked up to her as their boss and a symbol of authority.

The thought cast a light on the dark path she had been threading since last night.

She unlocked the door of her glass-partitioned office and padded through the soft carpet to her highback chair.

Sitting, she switched on the AC, opened the bottom drawer of her rectangular wooden desk, and pulled out some documents needing her signature.

The sound of her office door opening made her look upwards.

Aminata stood at the entrance, her pretty face split into a huge grin. She wore a beautiful burgundy skirtsuit, matching peep-toe suede heels and held a flask of steaming hot coffee in her right hand.

"Well, somebody woke on the right side of the bed this morning," Binta said to the smiling senior customer service officer, one of the few bank employees she got along with. "What has you in such a happy mood?"

"Remember the client I told you I might bring in?" Aminata replied, stepping further into the office.

"How can I forget? You kept talking about what a big score it will be for us if he set up his account here." Binta smiled.

Her colleague nodded excitedly. "He's arrived, and he wants to speak to the manager."

"Why isn't he already in my office then?" Binta admonished lightly, her mood already brightening considerably with this news. "Show him in."

She planted her left hand on the desk, leaned in with a mischievous smile and said in a near whisper. "I just wanted to confirm that the account wouldn't be given to anyone else but me."

"*Bul worry,* Natta. I wouldn't dream of giving it to someone else. Now bring him in before he changes his mind, and there will be no account to give to anyone."

"Right away," she chirped, exiting with a flourish.

BETTING ON LOVE

Seconds later, Aminata returned followed by a tall, light-skinned young man clad in a starched white shirt and black cotton trousers.

The smile froze on Binta's face when she saw who it was, her body stiffening in shock. Unbidden, his name fell from her lips.

"Bass."

His facial expression transformed from genuine surprise into cool indifference.

"I guess it was too much to hope that our paths will never cross again," he muttered low, seemingly for her ears only.

"Do you know each other?" Aminata asked, looking from one to the other.

Bass nodded. "We were friends, once upon a time."

"Then I'll leave you two to get reacquainted," she said and left the office, closing the door behind her.

"Please have a seat," Binta said.

He pulled out a chair and sat opposite her. His gaze was still fixed on her, unmoving, unwavering, as if like her, he wanted to wake up and discover that this was only a nightmare.

"So, you're a manager," he murmured with the ghost of a smile. "You're really doing well."

Binta felt like a lab specimen trapped under a microscope with the intensity of his stare. She nervously brushed away the escaped tendrils of hair from her face, willing her hands to stop trembling.

He was absolutely the last person she expected to just walk into her office.

Yet, there he was, looking hauntingly familiar and strange all at once.

He appeared as uncomfortable as she was.

She needed to get herself together and make sure he didn't bolt.

It had only been three months since she began working in this bank. Driving clients away wasn't a practice she should engender if she wanted to keep her job.

She fortified herself with this thought and said in her most charming voice. "So, what can we do for you, Bass?"

"My mother set up a trust fund for me in a bank in England called Lexington," he replied, his tone matter of fact, his demeanour still aloof. "I want to open a fixed deposit account here and have the funds transferred into it. Aminata already told me she will be the one handling it."

"Yes, she is quite competent. However, let me reassure you that I will oversee the transactions to ensure everything is done accordingly. Are you familiar with the process?"

"Not really and I know we have to talk about it at length, but I really need to get going now to avoid being late for work," he explained as he rose from his seat. "We can discuss the details when I come back."

"We can have the discussion over a meal if you like," she suggested, standing too. Being in an informal place might ease the tension between them and get him to relax in her presence. "There's a restaurant opposite the bank where we can meet after work."

"Are you sure?" he said quietly.

She was far from sure. Her first instinct was to scream no and run as far away from Bass as possible. But where to? And what would that accomplish?

Yet panic flooded her heart, a clear indication that dealing with Basiru Fall was the last thing she should do.

Had her life ever been a bed of roses though?

She had to do her best to make sure the bank's clients were satisfied, and right now, this was the only way she knew how.

She nodded and smiled. "I'm absolutely sure."

He gave her a once over, eyes narrowing slightly before he replied. "Okay, I'll meet you there at 3 p.m."

She slumped back on her seat, sighing heavily as she watched him walk out of her office.

What the hell had she just gotten herself into?

CHAPTER TWO

Star Delights restaurant was fully occupied as usual. The regulars included bachelors who couldn't be bothered to cook for themselves and businesspeople who liked to conduct deals while delighting in good food.

Then there were the high school students who must have saved up for some time to afford to eat at such an expensive place.

Binta enjoyed their gleeful expressions as they devoured the meals they ordered. She doubted they had ever stepped foot in such a fancy establishment before.

She had chosen a corner table, wanting to be away from prying eyes and the boisterous teenagers. She was sipping from a bottle of Coke, waiting for Bass to arrive before she ordered.

The restaurant had become a favourite of hers since she began working at the bank because they prepared exquisite food. She usually ordered takeaway when she closed from work since she rarely found a proper meal at home.

Their Wi-Fi internet connection was another reason it was such a popular place to hang out. In this age of technology, one of the attractions that hotels and restaurants alike held was providing fast internet connection. It was a good marketing strategy that Binta couldn't help but admire.

The interior of the place was beautifully decorated. Glittering chandeliers hung from the ceiling, and the walls were adorned with the loveliest of murals. The beautifully executed paintings depicted the life of a typical African village. The women who wake up at the crack of dawn to pound coos while carrying their young on their backs. The flowing streams populated with girls filling their pots with water from its depths. The farmers toiling tirelessly on their fields of land even when the scorching sun was at its peak.

Binta had never visited any of the villages in the country's interior. Still, these works of art imprinted a picture in her mind of what they would look like.

When she had been buried in work earlier, it had been easy to keep her thoughts from drifting to last night. But sitting in the serene confines of the restaurant with nothing to serve as a distraction, she was helpless to stop the feeling of melancholy that assailed her.

"Your parents didn't want you, and we took you in out of pity... If we had known you would turn out like this, we would have left you in the wilderness to rot."

The offensive words spoken by the woman she'd always thought was her mother reverberated in her head like the ricocheting sound of gunshots.

She leaned back against her seat and closed her eyes, exhaling shakily. Who were her parents? Where were they? Why did they throw her away as if she didn't matter? Did they know she was alive? Did they even care?

"Ready when you are, Ceesay Ngarri."

The deep baritone of Basiru Faal snapped Binta out of her reveries. She opened her eyes only to find him seated opposite her, looking at her closely as if he was trying to decipher what had been on her mind. She had been so absorbed by the tormenting questions running through her head that she hadn't been aware of his arrival.

Now that he was here, she was plagued with a different set of troubling questions. What on earth made her think she could handle this meeting? What was she going to say to him if he brought up their past?

"Might I ask what you were contemplating so thoroughly?" he interrupted her thoughts again.

"Just work stuff," she lied smoothly. The truth had nothing to do with him.

A smiling waitress approached to take their orders.

"Bring me a plate of super kanja and a bottle of Malta," she ordered.

"The local dishes they prepare here are to die for. *Nexh rek lenj def*," she added, addressing Bass.

"Then I'll have a plate of benachin. I want the red one and a glass of Wonjo," he said to the waitress.

"Coming right away," she told them and sauntered off.

Binta turned her attention Bass, marvelling at the hand of fate conspiring to bring them together again.

"You've changed, Bin," he remarked, settling back against his seat.

A sharp emotion shot through her at the sound of the nickname that only he used to call her.

It seemed like just yesterday when they had been the best of friends. But the harrowing memory of the disastrous way that friendship had ended was still vivid in her mind.

"I was about to say the same about you, Bass," she replied evenly, none of the frustrating emotions showing in her voice. "But then five years' *time bu barri lah*. Change is bound to happen."

His expression softened. He almost looked like the jovial boy she had known in high school and not the unapproachable stranger he was today. "You looked as if you had seen a ghost when I walked into your office."

She held his gaze. "It had felt like seeing a ghost. *Dama over surprise sah*. What have you been up to, Bass? Where have you been?"

He hesitated, looking down at his hands before bringing his eyes back to her face. He was clearly reluctant to talk about his life in the five years they'd been apart, and for reasons unknown, she found herself wishing that he would tell her everything. She hungered for any detail of his life that she could get.

After a period of silence, he began to speak in a quiet voice. "I had transferred to Cape Town University in South Africa. It's where I did the last two years of my BSc in Physics and Mathematics. After graduation, I returned to the country and taught at various high schools in the interior for two years. I've been teaching at our alma mater, Nusrat, since last year. That's about it."

"So, you did become a teacher, after all."

"Much to my parents' eternal disappointment," he qualified with an exaggerated sigh of mortification.

She smiled, thinking that his stubbornness hadn't reduced one bit. "I bet they said it's just another one of your rebellious exploits to annoy them."

He grinned at her wise summation. "You still know my parents so well."

"*Yaa gena hamneh* I was terrified of them, Bass. It is not likely that I would forget them anytime soon."

They both laughed.

Just like that, the tension dissolved between them. Right then, Binta seemed to have her best friend back, and the feeling was powerful enough to ease the heavy apprehensive weight she carried.

The smiling waitress headed their way carrying two dishes in each hand. She was accompanied by another who held their drinks.

"Here you go," she said, lowering them on the table. She took the drinks from her colleague's hands and placed them beside the plates. "Enjoy your meals."

"Thank you," Bass said to them with a smile.

"I hope it is as good as you said it will be," he said to Binta when the waitresses had gone.

"You'll soon find out for yourself. Dig in," she urged, ignoring her meal to watch him taste the attractive looking benachin.

He scooped the cooked rice, and a piece of roasted meat on his fork and the food disappeared in his mouth. The moans of pleasure that emanated from his throat as he chewed on noiselessly had Binta grinning from ear to ear.

"What did I tell you?" she asked her expression one of smug satisfaction.

"This is heavenly," he commented on a sigh when he could speak again.

Binta picked her own cutlery and began shovelling mouthfuls of the delicious Super Kanja she had ordered. As they continued to eat in comfortable silence, her attention was drawn to the couple that occupied the table adjacent to theirs.

The young man and woman looked to be about her age. They were holding each other's hands, speaking in hushed tones staring at each other as if the rest of the world didn't matter. Their love for each other was evident to anyone who looked at them.

The sight proved too disturbing for Binta. She'd never indulged in romantic entanglements simply because they tended to be messy and ended with heartbreak.

Her life was hard enough.

She didn't need the extra relationship baggage. She couldn't trust anybody with her heart.

Once upon a time, five years ago, she'd been tempted by the man sitting across from her, but she'd resisted.

They'd stood on a bridge while he confessed that he wanted them to be more than friends.

She'd turned him down flat and disregarded the feelings he had professed to have for her.

The fateful night had haunted her dreams ever since.

Staring now at Bass as he devoured his meal, she wondered how things would have been if she had reacted differently.

Instead, she had lost the best friend she ever had. He hadn't wanted anything to do with her after that. He had cut all ties with her, and losing him had been the most painful experience in her life.

"Don't tell me you're thinking about work again," he teased, pushing his empty plate away and wiping his mouth with a napkin.

"I was thinking about you still having the biggest appetite of anyone I know. *Chopsa binga done,*" she said with a laugh, pushing away the dark memories of their past. "Some things just don't change."

He sipped at his Wonjo drink. "Nope, they don't."

"I assume your parents wanted you to follow in Abdul Aziz's steps and join the family business."

He nodded. "I told them my elder brother is more than capable and happy to be Dad's successor."

Bass's father, Alhaji Mustapha Faal, owned a prestigious shipping company founded by his ancestors. It had been in their family for generations, passed from father to son.

It was the source of their immense wealth, but Bass had never shown an interest in the family legacy. He had always talked about following his own path.

She placed her spoon down and began to sip from her bottle of Malta.

"I can imagine that didn't please your father," Binta said, thinking about the rigid and uncompromising man.

Bass shrugged. "My life is my own to live the way I want to. I'm hoping he'll understand that one day. Teaching has always been my passion, and I would be doing myself an injustice if I chose a different path. But enough about me," he said on a dismissive note. "I want to know what you have been up to."

She interlaced her fingers on the table.

"It has been pretty uneventful," she began on a sigh. "After the WASSCE results came out, I enrolled at the university with a government scholarship. *Hamnga* how difficult studying at UTG can be. The ensuing four years were pure hell, but it was worth it at the end of the day. I have a job that I love with handsome pay. I don't need to rely on anyone anymore because I am fully capable of taking care of myself."

"I never doubted you for a second, Bin," he spoke softly. "Speaking about your job, however, I think it's time we talked about the matter that brought us here in the first place."

Binta sat up straight, mortified that the entire matter had slipped from her mind.

"The process isn't complicated at all," she stated. "All you have to do is give our correspondent bank address to your overseas bank. Then the funds can be transferred to the fixed deposit account Aminata is going to set it up for you."

"You are right. It sounds simple enough. *Baxhna*, I will get right on it."

"You do want this money to be invested, don't you?"

"Definitely, yes," he replied without hesitation. "I don't have any intention of withdrawing those funds any time soon. I haven't yet figured out what to do with the money."

"Spoken like a wealthy young man," she teased with a smile, her eyes glowing with a joy she hadn't felt in years. She really did miss him.

"I am not wealthy, my parents are," he hurried to correct her as he always did. A humbler creature than Basiru Fall didn't exist. "I am nothing but an over-worked and under-paid high school teacher who lives in a decrepit one-bedroom apartment. If I'm not careful, the whole thing will crumble around me one of these days. I seriously have to move, Bin."

She burst into laughter. He was as incorrigible as ever.

"That reminds me. I'm moving into an apartment I rented a month ago, so I really must go now. All my furniture will be arriving tomorrow, which means I have a lot of cleaning to do."

Bass signalled one of the serving waitresses over to their table. He was about to pay the bill when Binta stopped him.

"I invited you, remember? Let me handle the bill."

"Fair enough," he replied with an easy shrug.

Binta pulled out crisp hundred dalasi notes from her handbag, paid the waitress and tipped her generously.

"So, you've finally left Bundung," Bass remarked as they stepped out into the busy street.

She shook her head. "The compound I'm moving into isn't even very far from my old neighbourhood," she told him.

She had done that to assure her parents that her intention wasn't to cut ties with them. It was sardonic considering that was exactly what she was going to do now. They couldn't have made it more explicitly clear that they didn't want to be in her life.

Bass flagged down a taxi, and they got into the backseat.

"Where to?" the driver asked. He was a middle-aged man with a dark complexion and a stocky build.

"Give him the location of your house," Bass instructed. "He'll take me to mine once you've reached home."

"Bundung," she addressed the driver, "make a right turn when you reach the third junction after the borehole market."

"That's One Hundred Dalasi," the driver said, resuming his driving.

"No problem," Bass said to him and settled back against the seat.

Sitting in such proximity with him caused goosebumps to form on her arms. She was aware of him in a way that she never had before. Excited and terrified by the electrifying attraction she felt towards him, the car couldn't have been running fast enough. She was eager to get to her destination.

"How's Sira doing? The last time we spoke was before she left for Madrid," she asked about his younger sister.

Striking up a conversation would speed up the travel.

He smiled affectionately as he talked about his sister. "Bin, Sira got married."

"She did what?" she gasped, biting back a laugh of disbelief. "When did that happen? Who is she married to?"

He scratched his head, grinning broadly at what he obviously considered an impulsive act by his cherished little sister.

"It happened last year. She fell in love with a fellow university student in Madrid. After six months of being in a relationship with this guy, his name is Kebba, by the way, she informed us that they had decided to get married."

"And your father didn't object to this?"

"My dad doesn't know how to say no to Sira if his life depended on it. He gave them his blessing and a million-dollar mansion as a wedding gift. My mum almost had a heart attack, but she's fully on board now. Kebba seems like an okay guy. I threatened to do him bodily harm if he hurts my baby sister."

"I would be shocked if you didn't," she replied with a laugh.

Bass adored his little sister. Binta was two years older than her. She had grown to love the impetuous girl from the day her brother introduced them.

Binta gazed out the car window, observing the many different vendors that lined the streets of Serrekunda. Some of them were immigrants from the neighbouring West African countries selling fruits in stands. Others were women selling snacks like baked cakes and home-made pies, the source of income they relied upon to feed their families.

Commuters from work stood in clusters waiting for vehicles to take them home. In their colourful uniforms, energetic school students trudged around with their friends, chatting animatedly as their dusty feet ate up the distance.

She stared at her entwined hands, Bass's presence affecting her in a way she couldn't fathom.

Had it really been five years since she last saw him?

Sitting beside him in the back seat of a taxicab and chatting about his wayward sister as the world sped by made it seem as if no time had passed at all. And yet it was not so difficult to believe either.

Bass had changed a great deal. The cold indifference with which he treated her at the bank had rankled. He had let down his guard since then to even get her to relax despite her troubles. His physical transformation was even more astonishing.

His boyish good looks were replaced by rugged sexiness. His face was all angles and planes as his body was roped muscles.

She studied his profile as he stared out the car window. She noticed the way his broad shoulders and powerful arms stretched his white shirt. She swallowed hard, imagining him shirtless and at her mercy. Her eyes travelled down to his hands. She watched, fascinated as his long, tapered fingers silently drummed on his cotton encased thighs.

How would it feel to have those hands on her body? Touching her... caressing her... at her beck and call... ready to fulfil her every fantasy? The heat she felt spreading up her spine had nothing to do with the weather. It was pure lust directed towards a man she had rejected five years ago.

If that wasn't an unfortunate case of irony, Binta didn't know what was.

The car encountered a bump in the road and knocked her against him. Her hand landed on top of his, right above his thigh.

"Are you alright?" he enquired, turning away from the window, and facing her.

The words she wanted to speak out stuck in her throat. The intense look in his eyes robbed her of her ability to speak.

The proximity of his face, his wonderful scent, and sexy lips filled her with the longing to be kissed.

Wait. Did she really want her first kiss to take place in the backseat of a taxi?

Yet desperation made her want to close the distance between them. She needed to know if those lips tasted as soft and as delicious as they looked.

His sharp intake of breath told her he was as affected as she was.

When he placed his hand on her cheek and brought her face closer, she knew she was going to be kissed, and she couldn't give a damn about the time or place.

Her chest rapidly rose and fell in anticipation with every shallow breath she took.

As he leaned in to capture her mouth, the indiscreet sound of coughing made her jump back from him. She was thoroughly shaken and shocked by what she had been about to let happen in a taxi.

"We've reached your junction," the driver said, regarding her in the rear-view mirror. "Which is your house again?"

Clearing her throat, Binta put as much distance as she could between her and Bass before replying. "It's the fourth one on your right with the blue gate."

"So, this is going to be your new home," Bass murmured as the car glided to a halt beside the front gate.

His expression was unreadable at best and gave nothing away.

She nodded. "Yes, it is." She opened the door and stepped out of the car. "It was really good to see you after all these years, Bass," she told him sincerely, holding the opened car door.

His face was solemn as he replied. "Likewise, Bin. I'll come back to the bank once I have the funds transferred."

"Alright," she said and shut the car door.

She stepped back as the car sped away.

Pushing open the gate, she walked into the compound. It contained two rows of self-contained apartments that stood opposite each other separated by a spacious, tiled yard. The place c was quiet. The tenants mostly kept to themselves, and it was only on weekends that you see their children playing on the front yard.

The neighbourhood was the absolute opposite and could get chaotic with unrestrained, rowdy kids running around.

This didn't bother Binta, though. The commotion would be a small price to pay for the sweet freedom and peace of mind living here would bring her.

Her apartment was the second on the left row. She took out her keys from her handbag and opened the door to the veranda. Each tenant's porch was fenced in and secured with iron bars, providing a measure of much-needed privacy.

Binta used the other key in the holder to unlock the front door. A rush of excitement bubbled inside her as she stepped foot inside her rented apartment.

The satisfaction of knowing she wouldn't go back to the hellish place she'd once called home brought elation, tamping down the pain and confusion from last night.

She was not going to dwell on her past and everything that has gone wrong in her life. She was determined to wipe the slate clean and forge a new path; one that would lead to a successful and fulfilled life. Renting this apartment had been the first step.

This made her think of Bass, and the confusing feelings his re-emergence in her life stirred.

She shook her head, seemingly pushing thoughts of him at the back of her mind.

Her views about love and relationships hadn't changed in the last five years. If nothing else her resolve to stay away from anyone that might give her heartbreak had only strengthened after everything she discovered last night.

As soon as her business with Bass was completed, they were going to part ways for good. Glad at the conclusions she'd drawn about the matter, she turned her attention to surveying her new haven.

The house smelled of paint and polish, the walls a peachy cream colour she had chosen. The tiled floors were coated with dust and dry paint droppings.

The single bedroom and bathroom were just off the living area, which had a built-in open-plan kitchen. The apartment was a little expensive for the size. However, since it came fully equipped with a modern kitchen, she wouldn't complain.

Binta ambled inside the kitchen, a smile playing on her mouth as her fingers ran over the smooth wooden counter.

She admired the sparkling brand-new utensils and cutlery she and Maimuna had bought yesterday, now housed in the cupboard shelves.

She retraced her steps and headed for the bedroom. Her newly purchased mattress lay on the floor with the suitcases her friend must have brought in the morning. She had also promised to drop by and help her arrange the furniture arriving tomorrow.

Maimuna was indeed a godsend.

Binta needed to clean the house first, however. Changing into comfortable clothes, she retrieved a bucket and mop from the kitchen and got to work.

CHAPTER THREE

The buzzing sound of an alarm clock woke Binta with a start. She reached out her arm and pressed the snooze button, silencing the irritating sound.

Tempted to go back to sleep, she didn't have the luxury.

The agency she had hired to deliver her purchased household materials would have their trucks over in a while.

Groggily, she rolled out of bed and headed for the bathroom.

After showering, she stood in front of the sink with a skimpy towel tugged underneath her armpits and faced the wall mirror.

Her reflection stared back at her. The lovely angular face of a twenty-four-year-old young woman gifted with dark slumberous eyes, accentuated by high graceful cheekbones, a pert nose, full cherry lips and an ebony skin so dark it sparkled.

Removing the hairband holding her short, coarse hair, she picked a detangling hairbrush and tugged the unruly sable-coloured mass until the knots loosened.

Pulling the hair into a low bunch, she rewound the hairband into place, guaranteeing it wouldn't be a nuisance when she was busy.

Minutes later, she sat on her tiled kitchen floor, enjoying a solitary breakfast of buttered bread and hot coffee, dressed in faded jeans and a black sleeveless blouse. She drained the last dregs of coffee from her mug.

An insistent knocking began to resound on her front door. That had to be Maimuna.

Smiling, she got up from the floor, placed the mug on the counter and rushed to let her friend in.

Shockingly, Bass stood at the threshold when she opened the door, not Maimuna.

Her heart leapt to her throat at the devastating sight he presented. He was dressed in snug black jeans and a matching T-shirt with a brown duffel bag swinging from his left shoulder.

"What are you doing here?" she bit out through gritted teeth.

"Good morning to you too," he drawled, ignoring her question, and walking right past her and into the apartment.

She clicked her door shut and turned to face him, trying, and woefully failing to tear her eyes away from his magnificent form. She watched as if enthralled, as he carelessly flung his duffel bag on the floor.

"Nice place," he commented, his eyes travelling from one corner of the empty sitting room to another. "Although I believe it would look much better after it's furnished and decorated, don't you think?"

She leaned back against the door, heart thumping wildly at what she could only call anticipation of the unknown. "Bass, I am about to have my hands full here, so I really don't have time for house calls. If there is anything you wish to discuss with me about your bank account, come to my office on Monday. Otherwise, I would really appreciate it if you could leave."

"Bin, is that how to treat a guy who has come to offer you his services for free," he chastised, slipping his hands into his trouser pockets.

"What services?" she asked, puzzled.

"To help you set up your new home of course," he replied cheerfully, the alluring smile on his face taking her breath away.

"A friend of mine is coming over to help."

"Who would take care of the heavy lifting?"

"I've hired people for that," she told him firmly.

"An extra pair of hands couldn't possibly hurt," Bass said. "Are you trying to get rid of me?"

Binta was saved from having to answer by the sudden ringing of her phone. She fished the vibrating gadget from her pocket. She glanced at the caller ID. Maimuna.

"Hi, Mai," she spoke into the phone. "Are you on your way over?"

"Bin, I'm so sorry," she gushed out. "I won't be able to make it today. *Suma* boss has called for an emergency meeting to go over our upcoming presentation for the umpteenth time. I swear the man is the Devil incarnate. Who calls for a discussion on a Sunday?"

Maimuna worked for an advertising agency. She had an impossible boss who ruled with an iron fist.

"Don't worry about it," she hastened to reassure her friend. "Understand *naa*. We'll talk later."

"I'll come over the moment I'm free. Take care."

"You too," she hung up and put the phone back in her pocket.

"What did your friend say?" Bass asked.

"Maimuna won't be joining us," she replied in resignation. "She has somewhere else she needs to be."

"It's good that I'm here."

"Lucky me," she muttered under her breath.

The unmistakable sound of rumbling engines signalled that the trucks have arrived, which brought an end to the discussion.

Binta didn't have the time to debate over the reasons he should stay or leave.

Outside, four men emerged from the twin giant vehicles. They were dressed in blue overalls with Ideal Movers' logo sewn into their breast pockets and caps. The agency specialised in delivering their customer's goods from the stores of purchase to their homes.

The agents introduced themselves to Binta and Bass. They opened the trucks, and she checked whether all her stuff had been brought. After verifying that everything was in order, she didn't waste any time setting them to work.

Binta collaborated with the men, labouring side by side with them all through the morning and well into the afternoon.

Comradeship developed between Bass and the agents in the few hours. They carried and positioned the heavy furniture and electronic appliances around the house together.

Not surprising. His easy-going nature ensured he could make friends anywhere.

BETTING ON LOVE 51

She laughed at the ridiculous jokes they threw at each other as she supervised their work. She had a vision of the way she wanted her home to look.

By the time the men arranged everything to her specification, her dream had materialised into reality.

Menial work done, the agents departed, leaving Binta alone in the apartment with Bass.

She tried not to let this bother her, stubbornly refusing to look his way.

He worked by the wall, installing the flat-screen TV and the accompanying digital satellite receiver.

"*Bai ma dem hol* whether the refrigerator is working correctly," Bass told her and went into the kitchen.

As she hung the last curtain onto its holder, the young married couple who lived in the opposite apartment dropped by. They introduced themselves as Mariama and Babucarr Sallah and welcomed Binta to the compound.

"*Lee purr yow lah*," Mariama said with a smile, handing Binta a bowl of rice and chicken stew. "I figured you might be too busy to cook lunch."

"*Jere jeff y*," Binta replied. "I really appreciate it."

"Don't mention it," Mariama waived it off. "Don't hesitate to call on us if you need anything."

Bass was still in the kitchen after the friendly couple left.

"We have lunch," Binta shouted, placing the bowl on the centre table.

"Great! I'm starving," he shouted back. "I'll be out in a minute."

She decided to rush to the shop and buy refreshments before Bass completed whatever task he was undertaking.

Binta re-entered the house only to stop dead in her tracks at the vision that greeted her.

Bass had taken off his shirt.

Why did he take off his shirt? She leaned against the door frame, staring at his magnificent figure.

His back glistened with sweat from the hard labour he had been doing.

She continued to watch, swallowing hard at the way the muscles in his arms bunched up as he placed framed paintings she had bought in a local tourist market on the wall.

His skin was flawless, utterly without blemish. The need to put her hands on that hard male body rose like the violent waves of an ocean on a high tide.

She wanted to reach out and trace the trickles of sweat running down his back, to lick them off his body right before they disappeared in the waistband of his low hung jeans. Those jeans that accentuated his tight butt and long legs in a way that had her sensual imagination running wild.

Her mouth went dry.

Hell, it seemed all her body's moisture rushed and gathered at her core, leaving her throbbing, and yearning for the unattainable. Her desire for him was getting more potent than her will to stay away. How long will it take before she gave in to it?

She was still devouring him with her eyes when he put the last framed painting on the wall and looked in her direction.

His gaze heated, filled with unadulterated lust, effortlessly holding her captive under his sensual spell.

She was unable to move or even breathe.

His eyes dropped to her chest, focused on the swell of her breasts.

Her nipples hardened under his dark brazen look. She inhaled sharply as his tongue darted across his bottom lip. The image of their aborted kiss flashed through her mind. The need to taste his lips became a physical ache, sharp and constant.

"Where did you go?" he asked, eyes returning to her face.

With a herculean effort, she cut through the fog of desire in her head and stepped forward. She extended her hands, showing him the soft drinks she had purchased.

"I went to the shop to buy these," she said breathlessly. "Thought it will be nice to have something cool to drink after lunch."

A SMILE OF PURE SATISFACTION played around Binta's lips as she lazed on her soft carpet beside two empty bottles of Coke. Bass was stretched out on her black leather sofa with one hand over his eyes, seemingly exhausted.

"That was a nice lunch," he drawled.

"I wouldn't know," she remarked with a grin. "You ate all of it."

"That's a bit of an exaggeration, Miss Ceesay. You had your fair share."

"I still haven't thanked you for your help, Bass," she began softly, "you've been incredible..."

Was that the sound of snoring?

She rose from the floor to take a better look at him. She removed his hand from his eyes and placed it gently on his side. He was fast asleep, the rugged features of his face re-arranged into a mask of contentment. She remained beside him for a while, watching him sleep with a look of tenderness.

Binta took another bath and paid her amiable neighbours a visit, deciding it would be best to let Bass relax.

Mariama and Babucarr were thrilled to entertain her in their lovely house. They had three-year-old daughters, the cutest twin girls she had ever set eyes on.

She chatted animatedly with the gregarious couple and played with their irrepressible little girls.

Darkness had descended by the time Binta went back to her apartment. She found Bass sitting in an armchair, his duffel bag on the floor beside him. He had obviously showered and changed. He had on a different pair of jeans, a dark blue shirt, and an unbuttoned coat.

"I hope you haven't been waiting very long," she told him. "I was just in the opposite apartment."

He shook his head and stood up. "I slept like the dead. Would you mind if I leave behind the clothes I had on earlier?" he asked, gesturing to the duffel bag.

"You just want another excuse to come back, don't you?"

He held up his hands. "You got me."

She laughed softly. "Leave the clothes here. I would have them laundered and ironed for you. It's the least I can do to repay all the help you've given me today."

"It was my pleasure. It's high time I went home," he remarked, glancing at his wristwatch.

"*Bai mah* put on something heavy and see you off." The cold had set in with the night.

She walked into her bedroom, grabbed a jumper from her wardrobe and hurriedly put it on.

She left the compound first. Her skin prickled with awareness as Bass came out and stood beside her, the sound of his even breathing, giving her an inexplicable sense of comfort and fear at the same time.

The street was illuminated by lamps lit in the compounds and shops that lined it. Most of the residents were indoors, seeking the warmth of their homes in the face of such disagreeable weather. The howling of the wind and the occasional roar of a passing car were the only sounds that disrupted the serenity of the night.

She pulled the hood of her jumper over her head as the biting cold made her shiver and zipped it up to her neck. She stared at the tall and silent man standing beside her.

Following the direction of his gaze, she saw that he was looking toward the bridge of Bundung. She swallowed hard, knowing full well the significance that bridge held for both.

It used to be their favourite place in the world when they had been friends. It was also the place where everything fell apart, where the solid rock that had been their friendship disintegrated into dust.

"You live much closer to it now," he remarked lightly, eyes still fixed up ahead as he began to walk in that direction.

Still standing, she released a frustrated sigh and slipped her hands into her jumper pockets.

"Where are you going?" she whispered as the distance between them began to lengthen.

"To the bridge of course," he replied over his shoulder. "I haven't stepped foot on it in ages.

"Shouldn't you be heading home now? It's getting chillier by the second."

"Are you coming with me?" he asked, stopping short and turning to face her, ignoring her words.

She inhaled sharply, desiring to go with him and wanting to heed the dictates of her mind, which strongly warned against it.

Desire won in the end as it rarely did with her. Her eager legs ate up the distance between them, and she fell into step beside him.

As they walked, a sense of déjà vu swarmed her feelings.

Memories filled her mind.

They used to stroll through these streets of Bundung on nights like this. His friendship had meant the world to her. It had kept her from breaking down when her situation at home had been horrible.

Enrolling into Nusrat Senior and Secondary School was the best thing to ever happen to her. There, as a reserved sixteen-year-old sophomore student, she'd met Basiru Faal.

Despite the amiable smiles and easy-going nature of her classmates, she'd been wary of making friends. Although she was never standoffish or treated them with discourtesy, she had kept the interaction between them at a minimum.

Working hard and producing excellent results had been her only goal. She'd known if she wanted to escape the misery her parents put her through daily, she needed to concentrate and excel in her education.

She could then secure a good job in the future.

She hadn't wanted to have relationships of any sort. Forming bonds led to problems and disappointments, and these were distractions she couldn't afford.

Or so she'd thought.

Everything changed the moment a charming and handsome grade-twelve senior decided he wanted to be friends with her. Bass would not be deterred by her cold and unapproachable façade.

With surprising patience and iron-clad determination, he'd slowly worn down her defences.

"Forming bonds don't have to deter your learning," he'd said.

And had proved it too.

His friendship had contributed to her educational success and had made the experience of high school a marvellous one.

Being in grade twelve meant Bass had been preparing for the West Africa Senior Secondary Examinations. He had even left his parents' Villa in Senegambia and moved into the student quarters in Nusrat.

Those were rooms the principal often allowed some of the boys in the twelfth grade to reside in to study well without the distractions their homes provided.

Despite his dedication to his studies, Bass still made time to be with her. He was always there when she needed him.

She had trusted him implicitly. Although she never discussed her tribulations with anyone, she never hesitated to confide in with him.

Whenever he sensed her sadness, he would come to her house at night and take her strolling.

Careful to make sure nobody saw her leaving, she would slip out of the compound only to find him waiting for her at the gate. Hand in hand, they would traverse the length and breadth of Bundung and always ended at the bridge.

By then, her mood would have considerably brightened, and they would chat and laugh the night away.

Binta twisted her lips in a sad smile as they ascended the bridge, reluctant to leave the joyful memories.

The precious bond she and Bass shared had brought her happiness, and since the day that bond broke, a giant hole had formed in her heart that nothing had been able to fill.

She leaned against the railing of the bridge, her palms curled around the cool metal.

Bass stood next to her, his fingers almost touching hers, eyes scanning their surroundings.

Tempted to bring down her walls and let Bass into her life again, her self-preservation instincts strongly warned against this.

Besides, she wasn't sure what he wanted from her.

"This is where you did it," he spoke the words as if they were wrenched from him, his hands tensing against the metal barrier as he stared at the murky water churning underneath them.

Binta's heart tightened in her chest, knowing what he was talking about but she asked the question anyway. "Did what?"

He gazed at her, and the look of utter anguish in his expression was almost her undoing. "I told you I loved you, Bin," Bass said, "and you basically spat in my face without flinching."

"I didn't have a choice," she breathed the words, the howling wind whipping against her face.

"You could have chosen to give me a chance," he bit out. "How about that?"

"I had just finished high school. My primary goal was to enrol in university and get my degree. I didn't want the distractions that relationships bring," she pleaded with him to understand. "You were my best friend, and I didn't want that to change. The last thing I ever wanted to do was hurt you. I was honestly afraid of losing you if we began dating."

"I tried to make you understand that my feelings for you were too strong for me to be content with being your friend," he countered, eyes blazing into hers. "That's why I ended our friendship and cut all ties with you. I needed to forget you and staying away had been the only way to achieve that. Do you want to know how that turned out?"

Binta was afraid to ask. She gasped out in shock as he took a step closer and put his arms around her waist. His searing touch turned her legs into jelly. She held on to the lapels of his linen jacket to keep from falling, bringing him infinitely closer; so close that she could breathe in his heady scent.

"I've done everything in my power to erase you from my heart in the last five years, and I actually thought I had succeeded." His hot breath caressed her face in a way that made her shiver with want.

"But walking into your office yesterday and laying eyes on you again, brought all those feelings I thought had faded bubbling to the surface. The very heart you had ripped into shreds raced with joy upon seeing you. How do you do it? How do you manage to make me forget myself with just the mere sight of you? What do you have to say for yourself, Bin?"

She couldn't utter a single word, not when his mouth was so tantalisingly near to hers. The need to sample its hidden delights burned brighter than the harsh rays of the sun. Her breasts felt heavy, aching with arousal.

Without the slightest bit of warning, his mouth slanted over hers and ended her silent torment.

His tongue eased into her mouth's hot cavern, expertly tangling with hers in an erotic dance.

She arched against him. When her lust addled brain was capable of coherent thought again, she might regret this.

Right now, all she wanted was to give in to the exquisite sensations filling her body as he ravaged her mouth, claimed her in an earth-shattering kiss.

She responded with an ardour that tore an animal groan from him.

His wandering hands caressed the lower sides of her breasts, causing her nipples to tighten painfully.

The wild throbbing began in her pelvis and steadily built a rhythm, eliciting soft moans from her throat.

The blissful decadence reduced her world into a bubble of heat and pleasure. Bass was at the centre, kindling the embers of her desire into a blazing inferno of need that only he could satisfy.

He gently broke the kiss, breathing heavily, his hooded eyes banked with barely unleashed lust.

She lowered her hands from his coat, staggering back against the railing—overwhelming panic at the force of her own desire set in.

"I can't do this, Bass," she exhaled shakily. "I just can't.

Before he could do anything to stop her, she ran off. She didn't stop until she was safely in her apartment, as far away as she could get from Bass and the tempestuous emotions he had awakened.

CHAPTER FOUR

The delight Binta felt when Maimuna requested she accompanied her to a wedding reception was overwhelming. It would be the perfect escape, a temporary distraction from the emotional turmoil that clung to her like a band-aid.

"Whose wedding are we going to, by the way?" Binta asked her. It wouldn't do to go to a wedding without knowing the names of the couple.

Maimuna was flagging down a van heading for the Senegambia beach area.

"A colleague of mine called Omar Nyang. He's getting married to a lady called Rohey Jawara," she replied and added, "that van stopped. Let's hurry before it fills up."

Binta found it a tad challenging to quicken her pace in her pencil heels. Unlike Maimuna, she wasn't used to wearing this type of heels and was already regretting putting them on.

"Why did the van have to stop so far away?" she muttered, her gait a bit unsteady.

They entered the vehicle without incident, and it raced towards their destination at a breakneck pace.

They alighted at the Senegambia junction and walked the short distance to Kairaba Beach Hotel.

As they stood outside the hotel reception hall entrance, Binta gave her friend the once over.

Maimuna was dressed in an expertly tailored puffy-sleeved blouse and full-length skirt. The textile was of glittering golden colour. It looked enchantingly beautiful coupled with her gold necklace and matching bracelet and earrings. They were ushered inside by two teenagers dressed in sky blue ankle-length gowns and directed where to sit.

The *Ndanga* music resounding across the elegantly decorated hall was already cheering her up. She began to sing along to the well-known lyrics of Youssou Ndour's *Senegalais*. Guests kept arriving. Men were dressed in gorgeous tie-dye kaftans. The brilliance of the jewellery worn by some of the women outshone the hanging chandeliers. The bride and bridegroom hadn't arrived yet.

"So, what's going on with you, Bin?" Maimuna said to her. Her voice was muffled by the loud music.

Binta feigned ignorance. "What are you talking about?"

Her friend rolled her eyes heavenward. "Oh c'mon, you didn't exactly sound like someone in a good mood when we talked earlier on the phone. *Lan lah*? Talk to me."

Binta ran her fingers over her hair extensions, smoothing the long tresses resting over her bosom. "This is not the place to have that kind of discussion, Mai. The reason why I'm attending the wedding of two people I don't know is so I won't have to think about it."

BETTING ON LOVE

Maimuna was scrutinising her, and Binta had the instinct that she wouldn't like what her friend would say next.

Fortunately, she was saved by the arrival of the newly wedded couple. The music stopped playing. A group of *gaewels* stood on the dais. The sound of their melodious singing accompanied by the beating of the drums carried across the verse hall.

The bride looked lovely in a magnificent white flowing gown. She was hanging on the arm of her husband dressed in a white kaftan of a similar fabric.

At the same time, her bridesmaids trailed behind them in their marching pretty purple outfits. There was a smile of radiance on Omar's face as he stared at his new bride who looked equally happy as they sat side-by-side on the raised platform.

Binta felt a tug in her heart, a sudden yearning for the unfathomable clawing at her insides. She shook her head and forced a smile on her face.

"Don't they look lovely together?" Mai said on a sigh.

Binta leaned back against her chair and crossed one leg over the other. "Without a doubt."

From there on out, they were engrossed in the festivities taking place around them.

The *gaewels* were showered with cash and expensive jewellery as they sang the new couple's praises and to their respective families.

Binta delighted in the delicious food.

The music resumed playing when it was time for the couple to cut their multiple-tiered cake. The mellifluous voice of Pape Birahim filled the hall as all eyes were trained on the two people who had just promised each other a lifetime. Thundering applause resounded as they shared a piece of cake and a kiss.

The guests started going up to them to present their gifts. Binta and Mai were chatting about something when an average-looking guy dressed in a dark brown kaftan approached them with a tentative smile. His gaze was focused on Mai.

"You know you could be mistaken for the bride," he said to her, his eyes creased with playful laughter. "*Mashallah, jangha sanjseh ngah!*"

"*Bayil tonj*," Mai responded with a chuckle and then said to Binta, "this is Mustapha, a co-worker. Tapha, my best friend, Binta."

"So, you are the Binta I always hear about?" His gaze transferred to her.

Binta got up and shook his outstretched hand. "She does have the habit of rambling on about me. It's nice to meet you."

"Likewise."

"You two can keep each other company while I go hand over my gift, right?" Maimuna was already hurrying away before she finished talking.

Mustapha moved in to temporarily occupy the empty seat she'd vacated, his smile incredulous as he watched her walk away.

"Ah, so you're that Mustapha. I've heard about you too."

"So, she's mentioned me." He shifted his attention to her. "Maybe I am beginning to wear her down after all. Do you think I have a chance with her?"

Bin shrugged. "I really can't say. *Halehbi dafa over daegerr bopah*"

"*Lolou degalah*. I don't think I've ever met a woman as headstrong as she is." "You see. Her rejection of you isn't personal. It extends to every guy who's ever wanted her."

"Do you have any idea why that is?"

"I've asked a million times, but she always changes the subject, not that I would tell you if I did."

"I really do love her, you know."

"Then, don't give up."

THE NEXT MORNING, AFTER Binta and Mai had finished having breakfast, Bin sat on the counter and stared at her friend whilst she rinsed their mugs in the sink.

BETTING ON LOVE

"Mustapha seems nice," she said out of the blue. "And genuinely in love."

"They all are before they get you. It's the rule of the game."

"Mai *yowtamit*. I don't get your cynicism. I don't see any reason for it. Why can't you simply give the poor guy a chance?"

"Look who's talking. By the way, are you ready to tell me what's going on with you?"

Binta took a deep breath and recounted everything that happened between her and Bass from the second he stepped foot in her office.

"And I think I'm ready."

"Ready for what?"

"To let someone in. Who better to start with than the one who knows me best?"

A strange look took over Mai, and for a while, she stared into space and then without warning, she engulfed Binta in a hug.

"What was that for?" Binta asked as the embrace ended, not that she was complaining.

"I'm happy and proud. I strongly feel that it's the right decision. Bass is the real deal."

"And Mustapha might be too, but you wouldn't know until you give him a chance."

"Bin, I don't think—"

"What's the harm in trying, huh?" Binta pressed on.

Maimuna let out an audible sigh. "Fine, I'll think about it."

"You mean that?"

"Yeah, I really do. Now, let's go watch some make-up tutorials and practice on each other."

CHAPTER FIVE

The October sky was darkening with rolls of boiling clouds, hindering the sun from spreading its light. It was a stark grey Sunday afternoon at the Palma Rima beachside. The sea breeze was fresh as the waves churned violently back and forth.

A group of young men who had been engaged in a friendly soccer game began to disperse for fear that it might rain.

Bass bid farewell to his departing friends and walked over to a lone coconut tree. He leaned against it, kicking the intrusive particles of sand from his shoes as Sheriff, his closest friend came over and handed him a bottle of mineral water.

Like him, Sheriff was dressed in a polyester jersey and shorts, his arms and legs were covered with sand.

"Bass, we should get going," Sheriff said. "*Giss ngah asahman bi num mel*. It could start raining at any moment."

Bass uncapped the bottle of water and gulped down the insipid liquid. He rested his head against the rough bark of the tree, sighing heavily.

His friend shot him a knowing a look. "*Bull mah waxh neh* you are still stressed over Binta. I've already told you to get her out of your head. *Ndo bi* isn't ready for what you want."

"That's easier said than done, Sheriff," he bit out irritatingly. "You know how deeply my feelings run for her. And after our last encounter—"

"Is that what you're calling it?" he cut him off with a penetrating stare. "You mean when she ran off after you kissed her two weeks ago, aren't you?"

Bass was beginning to regret ever telling his friend about that.

Sheriff was hell-bent on convincing him that it would be in his best interest to stay away from Binta.

He couldn't argue the logic in his friend's advice, given her behaviour. Still, his conflicted heart just wasn't ready to accept it.

"It's difficult for her to let people in," he spoke in her defence. "She's scared of getting hurt."

"Are you honestly defending her?" Disbelief rang in his friend's voice. "*Hamnaa neh* you haven't forgotten the kind of pain her rejection caused you five years ago. I watched you fall apart, Bass, and there was nothing I could do about it. You transferred to a university on the other side of the continent just so you wouldn't have to see her face for god's sake!"

Bass's visage turned grim, his gaze riveted to the ferocious waves of the sea. He needed no reminder about the way Binta broke him apart. He hadn't been sure his feelings would be reciprocated, but he had at least been hoping to be given a chance to prove them. He had been prepared to wait for her if it was necessary. He hadn't expected his feelings to be discarded without a second thought.

The pain had almost driven him insane and the idea of continually seeing her when she joined him in the university even more so. Leaving the country had seemed like the best option, so he had taken it without much deliberation. Not being around her had helped, even fooled him into believing that she meant nothing to him anymore.

Nothing could have been further from the truth.

Bass's feelings for Binta burned bright and fierce.

He closed his eyes for a moment as the remembered pleasure of their shared kiss coursed through his body. He hadn't been able to stop thinking about her since then. Although, he'd made no attempt to contact her given their unpleasant parting.

"Bass, I have nothing against Binta," Sheriff said, cutting into his thoughts. "She was also my friend, and I liked her very much. I think she has feelings for you too, but her walls are there for a reason. They protected her against her parents, and she's unwilling to bring them down. Even though I don't think she needs them anymore."

"They deserve to be hanged for the hell they put her through." His anger spilled over his voice. "Who would have a daughter as amazing as Binta and treat her the way they did?"

"Only monsters, I guess."

Sheriff was right. Only monsters were that cruel.

Bass was filled with potent fury as the memories of the despicable things that beautiful girl suffered crowded his mind. They had refused to invest in her education, wouldn't buy her required school materials and even deprived her of lunch money.

She wouldn't beg anyone money to buy food, not even him. She had too much pride. Instead, she had found odd jobs such as laundering clothes for people on her free days and used the money to take care of her needs.

Bass had admired her strength and perseverance, the determination to work hard for the things she wanted in life, and her resilience never to be thrown off course.

The memory of one event haunted Bass.

A seventeen-year-old Binta had been saving up to get herself a beautiful outfit for an upcoming Eid festival. He vividly remembered her joy when he had accompanied her to pick up the finished sewn dress from the tailor's shop. She had laughed when he proclaimed she would be the most beautiful girl when she wore it on Eid.

On the day of the festival, her mother had seized the outfit, giving it to Isatou instead. She had ranted about punishing Binta for accepting gifts from men because Binta couldn't have afforded the expensive dress on her own.

Binta has cried in Bass's arms later that night, the only time he'd seen her in tears.

It hadn't been the loss of the dress which hurt her the most, rather, her mother's cruel actions and words.

The raw pain in Binta's voice had torn at Bass's heart, and he had wanted to strangle Musu with his bare hands.

"I know Binta has a lot of issues, making it a challenge to have a normal relationship with her," Bass told his friend. "But no other woman makes me feel the way she does."

"That's because you haven't given other women any real chance," Sheriff countered. "A part of you has always been holding on to Binta."

"I was fully committed to Naffie," he refuted firmly. Mentioning his ex-fiancé's name left a bitter taste in his mouth. "She ended our engagement the minute she realised I was never going to be the kind of husband she wanted to have. She didn't want to get married to a mere high school teacher."

"She wanted to marry the son of Alhaji Mustapha Faal and live a life of luxury that your father's wealth can give."

"Exactly. And to think I almost married her." Bass shuddered at the thought. He had dodged a bullet in the truest sense of the word.

"So, what are you going to do now?" Sheriff asked.

"I don't know, bro," he honestly answered. "The one thing I'm sure of is that we should get going before it begins to pour," he added, looking skyward.

Sheriff followed the direction of his gaze. The sky had turned completely black, and the wind had considerably picked up. They wasted no time in hurrying home.

THE FOLLOWING DAY, Bass made his way to the staffroom after teaching his last class in the afternoon shift. He felt the exhaustion that came along with lecturing on your feet the whole day weighing him down as he brushed off the chalk dust from his aching hands.

Mathematics was by far the hardest subject to teach. Most of the students found it either too dull to bother with or too tricky to tackle. His throat had gone hoarse from all the yelling he did to keep their attention on the lesson. He was eager to get home and relax.

Approaching the narrow corridor outside the staffroom, he saw an unexpected but more than welcome sight.

Binta was leaning against the staffroom door, a nervous expression on her face as her eyes studied the floor, obviously waiting for him. She looked utterly lovely in a creamy suit with matching trousers.

His breath caught in his throat as he continued to stare at her. His insides twisted with a knot of yearning that was as undeniable as the haunting emotions that filled his heart.

No matter what Sheriff said and whether he was ready to accept it or not, he wanted this beautiful and damaged woman with his entire being.

He couldn't force her into a relationship she didn't want, but he was damned if he wasn't going to do his best to convince her that they belonged together.

She didn't look up and see him until he had glided to a stop in front of her.

"I was told that you were teaching in class," she said by way of greeting. Bass didn't miss the way her voice slightly shook with what he could only interpret as nerves.

"The class is over. It was my last for the day," he said, tone wary, still surprised to see her here given the way she had run off on him two weeks ago. "Are you from work?" he added as an afterthought.

She nodded, her knuckles turning white as she clutched her white handbag. The worried look in her expressive eyes raised his hackles.

"Why are you here?" he asked, his voice coated with apprehension.

"We need to move to a more private place before I can answer you."

"Let's go to the field."

Placing a hand at the small of her back, he guided her down the cemented steps of the corridor. Their shoes' soles crunched the fallen dry leaves on the rich dark earth as they marched towards the school field. It was a vast open space that was entirely covered with grass during the rainy season. It was used for recreational purposes during recess, boasting both a basketball lawn and a football arena.

Bass was suddenly nostalgic. He and Binta had spent a lot of time in the field studying and engaging in other activities that were not so academic.

Concerned at her strange behaviour, he sent her a sideways glance.

Her gaze was focused on two giggling girls garbed in the white and navy uniform of Nusrat passing by.

"Miss high school?" he asked, seeking to distract from whatever it was that had her so on edge.

"Hell, no," her reply was swift in coming. "Don't get me wrong, being in this school was an unforgettable experience, but I was happy to move on."

They walked into the sparsely populated field. Bass could only see a few students occupying the stone benches. Some had their noses buried in books whilst others were chatting with each other. The air was crisp, and the grass was extremely green. The sun was peeking behind a smothering bank of grey clouds.

Bass led Binta to an empty stone bench at the far end of the field. It was as much privacy as they were going to get. They sat facing each other, and he waited for her to start talking. She abruptly stood up and began to pace in small circles.

"Tell me what's going on, Bin," he softly prompted.

The pacing seized, but she remained standing, staring down at him. Her gaze was intense, she seemed lost and confused to him, trapped in a conundrum with no hope of escape. He noticed the way her hands shook before they disappeared into the lacy pockets of her designer pants.

"You've been doing your best to ignore me," she said out of nowhere. "Aminata told me that you've come to the bank twice and asked not to see me."

It took a while for Bass to process her words as they hadn't been what he expected to hear. "I assumed it was what you wanted. Have you forgotten the words you said to me two weeks ago? You couldn't run fast enough to get away from me."

Her expression turned chagrined. "I regret what I did. It was childish, and I apologise."

He nodded his head, accepting the apology.

"I've been doing a lot of thinking."

"What about?" He was curious to know.

"About everything that's happened between us," she replied.

"For as long as I can remember, I've avoided getting involved in anything that might lead to causing me pain. *Halatuma won sah* how much you must have suffered because of me, Bass. I was selfish and a coward, too scared to put my faith in something as fickle as love. And now, after what I've discovered about..." her voice trailed off, she broke eye contact and stared down at the grass.

"Binta, look at me," he urged in a gentle whisper.

She did, and it took all his willpower not to visibly react to the abject pain in her eyes. "Tell me what you've discovered."

She exhaled erratically, blinking back the tears that filled her eyes, tears that she refused to shed.

"Musu and Babucarr are not my real parents," she said, her voice barely audible. "According to them, my birthparents threw me away and apparently I should thank my lucky stars that they were kind enough to take me in and raise me as their own."

Bass wished he could say that the news shocked him, but it didn't, not with the way Binta had been treated in that house.

"It still doesn't justify their cruelty towards you. There are lots of adopted children who never miss the presence of their true parents in their lives simply because of the enormous love and affection they receive."

"But it still explains a lot, Bass," she argued, a sad smile curving around her lips. "If both my adoptive and real parents couldn't even love me just a little, then maybe I'm the problem, not them!"

Bass grabbed her arms and sat her down on the bench. He placed his hand on one side of her face and forced her to look him in the eyes.

"Listen to me, you foolish woman," he commanded gruffly.

"I don't ever want to hear those ridiculous words coming out of your mouth again. You are insanely beautiful, both inside and out. Bin, you're the strongest

BETTING ON LOVE

and most hard-working person I've ever come across. Even though you drive me crazy more than any other human being, you're still the most adorable creature I know. I could go on and on all day about how incredibly amazing you are. Musu and Babucarr couldn't give you the love you deserve because they're heartless monsters. There could be a thousand genuine reasons as to why your real parents had to give you up. Don't just write them off without finding out the truth."

She buried her face against his hand and closed her eyes.

"I'm not sure how to do that or if I even want to," she whispered on a sigh. "Ever since I found out, I've made no effort to find them for the simple reason that the answers I'd be seeking might turn out to be my worst nightmares transformed into reality."

"I want you to promise that will change from today," he pressed. "If you don't find out what really happened, you'll be haunted with uncertainty for the rest of your life."

"You are right," she said with a nod.

"I need some sort of closure at the least. There's something else you should know," she added with a shy smile.

Bass's heart rate picked up at the sight of that endearing smile. "What is it?"

"It's high time I tried to overcome my fear of commitment," she said. "You've invoked some strong feelings that I don't know how to repress, and frankly, I don't even want to. I hope it isn't too late to give you the chance you'd asked for five years ago."

"It can never be too late, Bin," he murmured, overwhelmed with pure joy. "Tell me something, did you find my kiss so terrible that you saw running away as your only option?"

"You know it was anything but," she said. "It was better than I ever imagined my first kiss would be."

"First kiss, huh?" he teased, his blood heating up with desire as he stared into her beautiful eyes unabashedly clouded with want.

His gaze devoured her beautiful ebony skin, and he itched with the need to reach out and touch her. Her tongue darted out to moisten her full lower lip, and he went as hard as a rock.

He leaned in closer and whispered against her ear. "Ask me what's on my mind right now."

"What?" she breathed against his face.

"Kissing you again right here," he said and felt a shudder go through her as he nibbled on her earlobe. "Nothing will give me greater pleasure right now than to feel your delicious cherry lips against mine...to have your soft breasts pressed against my chest... caressing your silky skin—"

"Stop! Just stop," she groaned.

He grinned at the flustered expression on her face. "Was it something I said?"

"If you don't get me out of here this second," she bit out in a lust-roughened voice, "we will be arrested for committing indecent acts in front of high school students."

Bass threw his head back and laughed. He took hold of her hand, and they ran out of the field as fast as their legs could carry them. He did not want to give his students an education that wasn't part of the curriculum.

CHAPTER SIX

"Bin, are you ready for this?"

Maimuna's voice drifted over Binta as if from a distance.

She could make out the sense in her words but responding seemed to be a problem. Her eyes fixed on the white-washed cracked fence of the house she grew up in just as her feet glued to the ground.

Was it just her or did the place look more ramshackle than the last time she had seen it? The rusted front gate was hanging off its hinges ready to fall off at any second. It should be repaired before someone got hurt.

"Binta, did you hear me?" Maimuna spoke again, a little firmer this time. "Are you planning to remain standing here or are we actually going inside?"

What a question indeed.

Binta transferred her gaze to her friend and almost smiled at the worried expression on her face.

Maimuna looked stunning in the African attire she had on. The well-tailored full-length skirt and blouse became her most wonderfully. The flowery textile complimented her chocolate skin.

She should wear dresses like this more often and not only on Fridays for Muslims' sacred day.

Why was her mind occupied with such trivial matters?

She should be thinking about getting authentic information about her birth parents from people who loathed the very ground she walked on.

"I get that you are nervous and scared, but we have to go in. You promised Bass that you'd try."

Binta felt herself blossoming with warm sensations at the mention of his name like a flower opening itself to the rays of the sun.

The day she visited him at Nusrat had been the beginning of a fledgeling and fragile relationship. He was

BETTING ON LOVE

slowly bringing down her walls and burrowing himself into her heart.

She was always surprised at the incredible burst of uncontrolled happiness she felt in his presence or whenever she thought about him. She had to do this if only to fulfil the promise she made to Bass.

Nyu dem si biir," Binta said. Maimuna held out her hand, and she took it in hers.

They made their way into the compound, Binta's eyes darting around the sand-covered front yard. Isatou was hard at work under the orange tree laundering clothes. She ignored their greetings by pretending she didn't hear. She must resent Binta for leaving because she'd never had to lift a finger when Binta was around.

The corrugated iron sheet roof gleamed in the hot afternoon sun. The front door opened and Musu stepped outside dressed in a green *grande boubou* with a chewing stick hanging between her chafed lips. Her wrinkled face was scrunched with concentration as she secured her head-tie. Her expression turned hostile the second she laid eyes on Binta.

"What are you doing here?" Her hands were planted at her waist as she glowered at her.

Maimuna squeezed her fingers reassuringly, and Binta found the strength to speak up. "I have some critical questions to ask you about my birth parents."

She climbed down from the veranda and stood a few inches from them. "I don't have any answers to give you. I have already told you the only information you needed to know. You were thrown away, which can only mean that you meant little to them. Why would you want to know anything about them?"

Binta felt her temper igniting. "The only thing that should concern you is telling me everything you can remember about where I came from."

"And I have already told you I don't have anything to say to you about that," she shot back.

Isatou had stopped her laundering. She was leaning against the tree, watching the confrontation between Binta and her mother with rapt attention.

"We didn't come here to fight with you," Maimuna spoke up, her voice soft and placating. "The slightest clue we can have to help us in our search will be appreciated."

Musu bristled as if she were genuinely offended by Maimuna's polite words. Binta knew that the women spoilt for a fight with her every chance she got. "The only thing we found you with was the woollen blanket you were wrapped in. Babucarr came upon a wailing baby lying inside an open cardboard box in the dumping site and brought you home. I discouraged him against contacting the authorities so that we could keep you with us."

"*Lutaxh?*" she asked, her voice raw with emotion. "Why did you decide to keep me?"

Her expression was stoic when she replied. "I hadn't conceived yet and was afraid I never would. *Suma hamon neh* we were going to have Isatou, we never would have kept you."

Binta thought about how differently her life would have been if she had been found by good people or better yet if her parents hadn't thrown her away.

Musu hadn't told them anything that a search could be conducted upon.

"Was there anything else attached to the blanket? A note perhaps?" she finally asked.

"*Daeded*," Musu said with a firm shake of her head. "I doubt your parents wanted to make their identities or reasons known to whomever they hoped would find you."

The little ray of hope Binta had been holding onto shrivelled into nothingness at the sound of those words spoken so callously. A part of her had desperately wanted to discover something that would lead to finding her parents.

Musu turned her back on them and strode into her dilapidated house.

Binta noticed how the paint was coming off the walls as if it was being clawed off. Isatou went back to her laundry with a vengeance.

Maimuna led her out of the compound while disappointment crushed Binta's soul.

LATER IN THE NIGHT, Binta had a dejected air about her as she stepped into Bass's apartment.

The first time she had come to his place, she realised he had been exaggerating when he called the apartment decrepit.

It was a sparsely furnished flat which wasn't surprising since a bachelor resided in it. The walls were painted a deep blue, and the golden-brown curtains hung around gave the place a cosy atmosphere.

She wordlessly rushed into his arms, and he held her, waiting for her to tell him what the matter was when she was ready to talk. The silence that accompanied his understanding comforted her more than words ever could.

She buried her face in his neck, breathing his familiar scent. Relishing in the feel of her body pressed against his, some of her negative emotions dissipated.

She pulled back from his embrace because she liked it a little too much.

She slumped onto the leather sofa and stretched lazily, enjoying the delectable sight he presented towering over her.

He was clad in a pair of snug black khakis and a tight-fitting t-shirt that emphasized his broad shoulders.

The only sound in the room came from the insistent whirring of the ceiling fan.

She fought the urge to run into his arms again.

"I spoke to Musu today." She marvelled at how easy it was for her to now refer to the woman she had always called mother by her first name.

He joined her on the sofa. "What did she say?"

The hopeful expression on his face made her wish she had brought better news. She smiled at how ridiculous that sounded. She was the one without a family, not him.

"I was found at the dumping site. The only thing that accompanied me was the blanket I was wrapped in," Binta said, willing her voice to sound casual, to not resound with the concrete block of hurt lodged in her stomach. "There was nothing else that can indicate where I came from or who my parents were."

"I have to confess. *Foguma* we can trust Musu's words," he voiced out.

Binta didn't think Musu was trustworthy too.

"But what would she gain by lying about this, Bass?" she asked.

He leaned his head against the sofa.

"I don't know," he replied on a sigh, sounding frustrated. "But it doesn't mean we should give up."

She bent her drawn-up legs underneath her thighs. "What else can we do? We don't have the tiniest bit of information to help us forward."

"Maybe we should talk to Babucarr," he said. "He was the one who found you in the first place."

"It would yield the same results that speaking to Musu did," she pointed out. "If they are hiding something, he won't be the one to reveal it. I think he hates me even more than his wife does."

His expression hardened into a mask of anger.

"Did she insult you when you visited today?" His voice was taut, filled with tension.

The anger he felt on her behalf pleased her. She didn't see the need to upset him any further, however.

"No, she addressed me with as much civility as she could muster," even as the words left her mouth, Binta realised how close to the truth they were. "Can we talk about something less upsetting?"

The tight lines in his face eased away and his rugged features visibly relaxed.

"I suppose we can talk about the exciting project I'm working on." His smile was radiant.

"Tell me about it." Her interest was piqued.

"A non-profit organisation focused on helping the progress of education in developing countries is building a state-of-the-art science lab for Nusrat and four other high schools," his words brimmed with exuberance. "Think of all the ways this is going to advance science locally."

"It's a step in the right direction for this country," she commented, her fingers running over the smooth leather of the sofa.

"I know. My students are excited about it."

"And how many of those female students are crushing over their insanely hot teacher?" she teased with a smile.

"I wouldn't know," he replied smoothly, softly, his dark penetrating gaze holding her captive. "I only have eyes for one woman."

The seductive timbre in his voice and the scorching stare aroused her, made her ache for his touch.

She straddled his laps, her soft and sensitive core colliding with his shaft which slowly began to fill up and nudged against her now moist channel.

She moaned unapologetically as the clothes between them didn't diminish the delicious pleasure the illicit contact brought and firmly grasped his shoulder blades to maintain her balance.

"Do you know why I resisted your offer of a dinner date tonight?" she asked, eyes studying the tortured expression on his face. She revelled in the intense arousal that swirled in the depths of his eyes and the way his breathing had gone laboured.

He shook his head as if talking had also become problematic.

"I wanted you all to myself," she husked, her lips lightly trailing his jaw.

She loved the roughness of the recently shaved skin. That slight touch electrified her senses with desire. She bent down, snaking her tongue along the column of his neck. He shuddered, his hands clasped around her waist.

"Plan to have your wicked way with me, I see," he growled out, sounding breathless. His hands slipped inside her blouse, cupping her soft breasts, caressing the tender flesh.

The sweet bliss his hands brought filled her belly, tightened it with sensations that overwhelmed. Her mouth went dry and her wet channel clenched with need as his erection throbbed against her.

"Kiss me," he bit out hoarsely. "I need to taste you."

As their lips merged, Bass got more than he bargained for as the passionate woman in his arms kissed him with fervour.

The sounds he made showed he was reeling with an all-consuming hunger that drove him insane.

Her tongue ran along the contours of his mouth softly biting his lower lip.

He groaned and clasped her tighter to him, roughly caressing her luscious breasts. His arousal pulsed as if in exquisite torture and painfully restricted in his pants.

Binta was out of her mind with pleasure, drunk with the need for more.

Their tongues mated savagely, and her nipples elongated into hard buds as his hands continued to wreak havoc to her breasts.

She mindlessly ground herself against his erection and her feminine nub vibrated with the need for release more powerfully than ever.

She sighed into his mouth as her hand explored the hard wall of his cotton-covered chest. The guttural groans that emanated from his throat as she continued to grind against him filled her with feminine pride that she could give him this much pleasure.

His fingers circled around her erect nipples, twisting them roughly and she gasped deliriously, leaning against his touch.

"You taste as intoxicating as you smell," he breathed against her neck as he splayed it with soft kisses and bites.

Binta laid her forehead against his face, panting audibly, consumed with passion's fiery flames. Her body suffused with heat as much as craving.

Slowly, deliberately, her drenched channel slid along the hard length of his shaft, and Binta felt a mini orgasm racked through her frame. The pleasure was that intense.

She repeated the action, and they both groaned out in unison.

Bass bit her neck painfully in reaction to the fiercely potent sensations that gripped him.

"If you keep that up, I'm going to come in my pants," he ground out.

"That's exactly what I want," she stared into his deep, fathomless eyes as she said this, all the while rocking against him. "I want to drive you over the edge, Bass."

"You are a naughty girl," he hissed through gritted teeth.

She smiled and then it turned into a throaty moan as she felt the sharp pinpricks of delight travelling down her spine.

She covered his mouth with hers, sucking on his sinfully succulent lips, her hands gripping the back of his neck.

She was rough, wild, and utterly uninhibited as she gyrated against him, chasing that elusive release that was suddenly within reach.

"Come for me, Bass," she purred against his swollen lips. "Now."

"Bin!" he shouted out as spasm after spasm shook his body.

At the sound of her name, spoken so desperately as if his next breath had depended on uttering it, she followed him over the edge. Her moans were loud as her channel clenched violently.

Her heart raced so erratically that she feared it would burst from her chest. She felt her body stiffen against him as she rode out the indescribably burning sensations that filled her every pleasure receptor.

She sagged against him, feeling weak but immensely satisfied, a lazy smile curved around lips that still burned from his kisses. A contented silence descended upon them as their breathing slowly returned to normal.

"I want us to spend the next weekend in the interior," he said when he could talk again. "I booked one of the Mandina Lodges. Have you heard of it?"

She nodded, sitting up to face him in excitement. "Maimuna told me that it's the best luxury eco-resort in the country."

"So, you have no objection?"

"Objection?" Her voice rang with disbelief. "There's no way I'm objecting to a trip with you."

Binta gave him a soft kiss all the while smiling, feeling ecstatic. An entire weekend with Bass sounded like bliss.

CHAPTER SEVEN

Enclosed in the Makasutu Culture Forest was a private eco-tourism woodland reserve located in Kombo Central District of the country's West Coast region.

Mandina Lodges was a tiny slice of heaven, and Binta fell in love with it at first sight.

The mangrove creeks and forest reserve's breathtaking beauty made it a popular tourist destination and a favourite for honeymooners.

Bass borrowed his elder brother's Range Rover SUV for the trip. The sturdy vehicle was the most ideal when travelling to the rural area.

An hour on the road and they arrived at the resort at noon.

BETTING ON LOVE

The wooden walkway that led to the river lodges was surrounded by expansive greenery. It swayed under their feet as they crossed it.

The hut-shaped stilted lodges looked picturesque from afar, simple but wildly beautiful at the same time. Its light brown roof gleamed proudly in the afternoon sun.

The lower level sporting an outside deck was of two floors whilst the upper one housed an exceptional dayroom and an outdoor lounge. Its separate bedroom was impressive in its size.

The room's smooth wooden panelling made it spacious and airy. The ceiling was high and distended with a rotating fan hanging from it.

Sparsely furnished, it had a massive, canopied bed with a stool beside it, two huge silver flower vases and brown cushioned seats.

Bright white curtains were drawn back from the glass windows to let the breeze in.

After taking a shower, Binta dressed in a strapless knee-length silky violet dress and gold studded blazer.

Then, she went to the upstairs dayroom to wait for Bass to finish doing the same.

She stood on the exposed platform and ran her hands idly over the smooth ligneous railing.

The early November wind sent a chill through her, despite the sunny afternoon.

She felt attuned to her surroundings—the stark green of the mangrove trees and forest. The natural beauty of the still, silver waters all but took her breath away.

Footsteps announced Bass's presence before his hands slid around her middle, clasping her to him.

She leaned against his solid frame, sighing in absolute pleasure.

"This is the most beautiful place I've ever been to," she told him, smiling at the view. "It's so peaceful. You cannot help but relax, let your guard down and just be. Can you feel it? The calm that just calls to you?"

"The only thing I can feel right now is how hungry I am," he rumbled against her temple, his breath warming her skin.

She burst into laughter, turned around and led him by the hand. "Let's go feed you then."

WHEN THEY ARRIVED AT the Baobab Bar and Restaurant, there was an outdoor buffet, trays and bowls were filled with scrumptious looking local dishes.

Binta watched with amusement as the tourists tasted each delicacy before deciding which one to take.

She and Bass made their way over to the table. As Bass began scooping Jollof Rice on to his plate, Binta was drawn to the rich-looking *Domoda* soup. She ladled her plate with it atop the well-cooked rice.

After serving themselves, they headed for the *Bantaba*; the thatched shaded structure was tall and spacious, its earthiness appealing. Binta and Bass enjoyed their meal immensely, even striking up conversation every now and then with their fellow diners.

Feeling more relaxed than she could ever remember being, Binta found herself opening. She felt the ice she had surrounded herself with melting away. She felt happy, free and a little vulnerable.

After the lunch, a local troupe of entertainers from the neighbouring village came on stage. A performance of extraordinary dancing and drumming ensued.

Binta was caught up in the drums' primal rhythms, fascinated by the young male and female dancers' hypnotic grace.

Even as enraptured with the routine as she was though, she could feel Bass's gaze on her, soaking up the expression of joy on her face, silently devouring her with his stare.

Her blood sizzled with excitement, and her heart thumped louder than the thunderous sound of the beating drums. There was a sense of expectation in the air, mysterious energy that was careening towards an unknown zenith.

The uproarious applause that broke out when the performance ended was deafening.

Binta and Bass vacated the restaurant and strolled over to Base Camp at a languid pace.

The camp had a white viewing tower that stood tall and defiant, overlapped by two spiralling staircases.

Hand in hand, they climbed one of the stairs and ended at one of the three viewing raised platforms. She extricated her hand from his and moved away, suddenly needing to put some distance between them.

She felt like a tightly leashed storm on the verge of being let loose, so overwhelmed with emotions, she shook with them.

Now, this was a view worth savouring. She needed a temporary distraction. The entire reserve was laid out in all its stunning glory.

She took in the magnificent sight of the palm trees as their leaves rustled in the breeze, the never-ending *Manding Bolong* and the untamed beauty of the Savannah Habitats.

Her heart twisted and ached—nothing to do with her surroundings and everything to do with the man standing behind her.

Bass stood still, expression puzzled as if he was aware of the tempest brewing inside of her.

"Something's going on with you, Bin," he said. "Tell me what it is."

She slowly turned, her eyes running over the entire length of him before coming back to his face.

As usual, he was clad in simple jeans and T-shirt, hands buried in trouser pockets.

Binta stared at his face, gaze slightly resting on the rigid line of his square jaw before settling on his stormy eyes.

She felt the lure of his gaze in the deepest parts of her being, the yearning that resounded in their depths reflecting her own.

"I have this deep-seated need for you," she whispered, "this raw and fierce longing that seems to keep growing and nothing has ever terrified me more."

His expression remained guarded, unreadable. "That shouldn't scare you in the least."

"You don't get it, do you?" She sounded exasperated and anguished. "No one has ever showered me with the care and affection you so easily give. I wish with all my heart that I could just enjoy it and not worry about the consequences, but I'm unable to."

"Why not?"

"Because, Bass, I want you more and more every day!" she shouted in his face, eyes glazed over with conflicting emotions.

"I yearn for your presence, your laughter, the look of desire that lights your eyes when you stare at me, and your smile. God, how the sight of your smile pleases me. I feel like an all-powerful goddess just by putting one on your face. It actually hurts the way I hunger for your touch, your kiss, it is a raw and constant ache... it builds and builds until I feel as if I would die without it... as if—"

With a growl, Bass yanked her in his arms and claimed her mouth in a non-too gentle kiss, but Binta revelled in it.

Consumed with need as she was, she greedily kissed him back, needing the sweet taste of his mouth more than she needed her next breath.

Her moans of delight were muffled in her throat as their tongues entwined in a mating frenzy. She was enveloped by his heat, her breasts rubbing against the hard wall of his chest.

Bass's hands roamed the length and breadth of her shapely hips, pulling her tightly to his body.

The pleasure was delicious, blinding, and absolute. So intense, it was too much.

His scent permeated her senses, drugging her, making her hunger for him even more.

He groaned into her lush mouth, cherishing it with his lips and her heart swelled with rapture to the point of pain. Desperate for more body contact, she roughly ran her hands along his muscled back, ferociously digging her fingernails into his willing flesh.

As abruptly as it had begun, the kiss ended.

She turned into his arms, plastering her back to his front, her head contentedly resting against his chest.

Still breathing heavily, he kissed the top of her head and circled his hands around her waist.

"Everything you feel for me, I feel for you too," he said to her. "I always have, right from the beginning."

She took in his words as they both stared at the view.

Surely something that felt this good, this intense couldn't last. Or could it? Could the Fates finally be smiling down on her? Was it her turn to experience happiness? Or like any other good thing in her life, would Bass eventually be taken away?

However, what truly frightened her was the possibility that she might do something to ruin this.

Giving up control was not something she saw herself doing now or soon.

THE NIGHT extravaganza was in full swing as the evening set in. It was a grand affair, designed to entertain and enthral the guests.

The delicious aroma of grilled meat was heavy in the air. Lit torches' flickered, giving the atmosphere a mysterious feeling.

It was a crazy mixture of colour and glorious noise. There were talented fire breathers, ridiculous jugglers, and skilful acrobats.

Masqueraded in their red and white costumes, *Mamaparas* danced on stilted legs, as tall as jackal berry trees.

After they had helped themselves with the barbecued stakes, Binta and Bass leaned against a pillar, fully engrossed in the revelries going on around them.

The viewing tower's emotional scene had left her feeling wrung out, but she was now in high spirits.

Local dancers dressed in skimpy tops and round skirts of dyed fabric with white beads worn around their ankles were a sight to behold.

Energetically, they moved their well-formed bodies to the beat of the *djembe* drums. Their breasts jiggled, and their waists swayed as they danced around in harmony, their moves synchronised.

Bass regarded Binta with an amused look. "It seems as if you'd like to join them."

Binta hadn't even been aware that she'd been swaying to the drums.

She laughed, entwining her fingers unconsciously with his. "*Halatuma koh sah*. I am a lousy dancer."

"You can't be that bad."

She rolled her eyes heavenward. "I am worse than you can imagine."

"Bin, *yowtamit*," he urged, bringing his hands together as if in supplication. "Dance for me."

She held up her hands, laughing. "*Baxhna, baxhna*."

She let the drums' seductive rhythm and the beautiful melody of the local song take over. Her body began to move in no particular style.

As Bass clapped in encouragement, she grew bolder, her inhibitions slipping away.

It no longer mattered whether she was a terrible dancer or not. She just wanted to dance for the fun of it, not worry about the future but to live in the moment to the fullest.

"You might as well join in," she said, pulling Bass forward.

His smile was handsome as he twirled her around.

Binta sashayed her hips for his benefit, laughing at the comical expression on his face.

Holding hands, they danced in the sands, completely out of tune with the music and not giving a damn about it.

They were two merry souls dancing for their singular joy, locked in their own private universe where everything was of blinding colour and screaming sensation.

BINTA WAS ENCASED IN Bass's arms back at their lodge, hours later.

They both stretched out in the swinging hammock in the outer deck.

There was a full bright moon, its reflection danced against the calm river.

Away from the incredible noise of the festivities, birds and crickets' cries were loud in the air. Mosquitoes buzzed around in the distance.

"Did you apply the insect repellent I gave you?" Bass asked. The feel of his fingertips running over her hands almost made her purr with satisfaction.

"I did."

Their legs were entwined, her left cheek rested against his collarbone as she was lying on her side.

She loved being this close to him, touching him, his body heat suffusing her with warmth. She took his free hand and brought it to her face, kissing his knuckles.

Was she getting too addicted to this man?

The thought darkened her mood, so she pushed them at the back of her mind.

"What do you want out of life, Bass?" she suddenly found herself curious to know. "What would you consider your biggest dream?"

He was silent for a while as the hammock swayed beneath their weight.

"What most people want, I assume. Wife and kids, a beautiful home filled with laughter and love."

She sat up, regarding his face in the semi-darkness, her hands splayed on his chest. "Most people want immense wealth and fame."

A deep chuckle rumbled in his chest. "Fame and riches hold little appeal for me. They complicate life and frequently rub your peace of mind."

She bit her bottom lip in contemplation. "You want a simple life."

He covered her hands with his as he replied. "I would consider myself a fulfilled man if I'm lucky enough to be blessed with a life partner who will give me her unconditional love. A wife to raise children with, one who would always be by my side and support me through thick and thin."

Binta looked away as if Bass could see the expression on her face. His words hit an inner chord and invoked feelings she didn't dare examine closely.

"I have big ambitions, Bass," she found herself confiding in a quiet tone, "so many things I burn with the desire to accomplish."

She faced him again. His dark eyes bore into hers, scrutinising her.

"I can see myself climbing up the ranks of power at the bank and being appointed the general manager."

His lips twisted in a wry smile. "But you have no intention of stopping there."

She shook her head. "I hope to establish my own company one day, be my own boss."

"You don't like taking orders from anyone, do you?"

"I most certainly do not," she confirmed without hesitation.

"Well, I only hope that you won't be too posh for the likes of me when you're running your multi-million business empire," Binta could hear the grin in his voice.

She lifted her chin, all haughtiness. "Mister, I wouldn't even spare you a glance."

They burst into gales of laughter, and a lapse of comfortable silence ensued as they listened to the sounds made by the creatures of the night.

Something niggled at Binta.

With all his talk about the future and building a family, Bass hadn't made any insinuations about wanting Binta to be a part of it.

Did he want their relationship to culminate into something more, and if so, how did she feel about that?

CHAPTER EIGHT

The following morning was a sun-drenched Saturday, perfect for lazing by the poolside in comfortable loungers while sipping cool apple juice.

A sigh of decadent pleasure escaped Binta's lips as the golden rays of the sun caressed her ebony skin.

She was dressed in marching yellow shorts and a tank top, enjoying the sight that Bass made as he swam in the vast swimming pool in his trunks.

He was an excellent swimmer. His lithe fair body moved through the water with such agility, he could be mistaken for a sea creature.

The atmosphere was serene, relaxing, so unlike her rowdy neighbourhood or the hustle and bustle of Serrekunda.

The only sounds that disrupted the peace were the birds' calls and monkeys' chattering in the trees and mangroves. Everything here was natural, sublime and appealing to the senses.

A couple she recognized as guests from yesterday's festivities jumped into the pool together, splashing water on the tile floor. Their laughter resounded after them as they swam to the farther end of the pool. They were young, in their thirties perhaps, obviously crazy in love. They were probably newlyweds, she mused with a half-smile.

Her attention refocused on Bass as he swam to her side. He placed his wet arms on the tiled edge while his legs and lower body dangled in the water.

The sunlight transformed the droplets of water on his face into sparkling diamonds, and she felt her heart clench in her chest when he gifted her with a grin. This man was going to be her undoing.

She sat crossed legged, facing him, all her fears and worries fading away as she gazed into his eyes, wondering why he had such an effect on her.

He picked up his juice from the tiled floor and took a long sip, his Adam's apple bobbing as he swallowed. He placed the glass down again, his attention solely on her.

"Are you glad I brought you here?" he asked.

"Can't you tell?" she retorted, rolling her eyes at him. "This place is perfect. As impossible as it is, I honestly don't want to go home."

His expression turned contemplative, hesitant.

"Bin, I love that you're having a good time here but the fact that you don't seem at all disturbed by our failed attempts to find your birth parents before we came here worries me."

Binta stiffened, suddenly looking away. Her gaze rested on a couple of agile, black-furred monkeys, deftly swinging from one tree to another.

Her fingers closed around the hairband that secured her short hair, loosening it a bit.

What did Bass want from her? Was she supposed to put her life on hold for two strangers who had abandoned her?

"Didn't you bring me here so I could forget my troubles?" she bit out, her angry gaze swivelling back to him. "Would you prefer to see me moping around for people who probably don't deserve it? *Lolou nga buga mah def*?"

He shook his head in frustration, the look in his eyes earnest. "*Daeded*, of course not."

She folded her hands beneath her breasts. "*Kon*, what do you want?"

Sighing heavily, he climbed out of the water.

Angry or not, Binta was helpless to stop the bolt of desire that instantaneously shot through her body at the sight of Bass's dripping naked chest.

His skin glistened, the flat brown nipples making her mouth water. Her gaze was still riveted on them as he sat down on the lounger beside hers.

She wanted to leap at him, clamp her mouth over the tempting buds, experience how they would feel against her tongue.

What would his reaction be if she grazed them with her teeth or suckle them in passionate hunger?

Will it arouse him? Will he urge her on with groans of pleasure or maybe feel obligated to return the favour?

She pictured Bass's sensual mouth closing around her nipples, and she almost whimpered with need where she sat.

"Bin, for God's sake! Listen to what I'm saying," Bass demanded, cutting through the haze of her fantasies.

She snapped her eyes open and dragged in a shaky breath. What the hell was she turning into? "What were you saying?"

Bass ran a hand over his low-cut hair, a gesture that betrayed his annoyance at her. "I don't think you even want us to find your parents. Somehow, you believe not knowing what happened is better."

"Can you blame me?" she fired back, aware that she hadn't denied his words.

He picked up a fluffy white towel from a nearby stool and began to dry himself. "No, I can't. But as I've told you several times already, not knowing the truth will haunt you for the rest of your life. Bin, you must stop running away from the things you believe might because you pain. That is not the way to live."

Her anger returned in full force. She stood up and looked down at him, her eyes shooting daggers.

"Just because we're in a relationship doesn't mean that you get to tell me how to live my life," she dished out acidly, jabbing a finger at his face. "Yes, I took the decision to stop looking for my birth parents because I'm not really interested in finding out why they threw me away. I've been doing pretty well on my own and will continue to do so. If you disagree with my decision, that's your problem, not mine."

Hissing, she stormed away and marched toward their lodge, stubbornly refusing to reply as he shouted her name again and again.

Nobody was going to tell her how to live her life, not now, not ever.

BASS MADE HIS WAY UP the stairs of the dayroom, taking two steps at a time, his leather loafers heavy on the wooden planks. He stepped onto the platform and stopped short as his gaze fell upon Binta.

She wore black jean trousers and a white blouse, her neck adorned with a simple gold necklace. She stood under the shade of the palm-frond roof, arms crossed underneath her breasts, eyes staring straight ahead.

He watched her closely, his breathing almost stilling in his chest, the troubled expression on her face was a knife twisting in his stomach.

She seemed to be surrounded by an air of melancholy, and Bass was aware of the reason.

It didn't take a genius to figure out that she was thinking about the people who gave birth to her and seemingly threw her to the wolves.

No matter how much happiness she might have in her life, this would always cast a shadow upon it.

Even if it was the last thing he did, Bass was going to find her parents. But he couldn't bear to see her in any kind of distress so he was going to do it on his own and would keep it from her until he had results.

He could almost imagine how monumental her reaction would be when he finds them and tells her about it.

His lips curled into a smile as he walked toward her. It was a good plan, and he was glad to have thought of it.

"Binta," he called out softly.

She jumped at the sound of her name. Facing him, her expression turned guarded, "Bass, if you're here to lecture me some more—"

He placed a finger over her lips, effectively silencing her. "I didn't come here to bring that up. I'm sorry I did in the first place. You're right. It isn't my place to interfere."

Binta looked taken aback by his apology. She removed his finger from her mouth. "I need you to put this matter at rest. I want to move forward, not look back."

The sound of buzzing insects was loud around them. In the silver river banks that bordered the swamp, a couple of crocodiles were basking in the sunlight, their enormous mouths wide open.

"I've booked a private tour of the bush forest," Bass said, linking their hands.

"It's high time you did," Binta replied. "I have been dying to explore the lush vegetation and see more of the wild animals that live within it."

"Does that mean I have been forgiven?"

She grinned.

"That depends on how great the tour is," she said and laughed when he faked a crestfallen look.

Bass was still pretending to be crushed when Binta stood up on her toes and kissed the bridge of his nose.

His heart did a somersault at the natural display of affection. It was a sign he was winning over her heart. And he was grateful for it.

THEIR GUIDE'S NAME was Junkung Kujabi. He was a native Jola, residing in the neighbouring Kembuje village. He was of medium height with a muscled body. He had a dark complexion, thin eyebrows that sat above narrow eyes and a flat nose. He was jovial and seemed to know his way around the forest.

Holding hands, Binta and Bass followed in his wake like two eager schoolchildren.

They trekked into the heart of the forest, going through the lush Guinea Savannah.

They were surrounded by wild trees and shrubs. Shrouded with the secrets of ancient times, the forest hummed with a life of its own.

The atmosphere was a cacophony of sound, the cries of the various kinds of birds mingled with apes' chattering.

The rustling of leaves merged with the scurrying of squirrels along the tree branches.

Binta's gaze darted all over the place, wanting to take everything in all at once. The sunlight streamed through the trees, casting shadow circles on the ground.

Once she and Bass fell in step with their guide, he told them some fascinating oral history about the place.

"My grandmother used to tell me frightening tales about the *Ninkinanka* that lived in this forest," Junkung said to them.

Binta furrowed her brow. "What's a *Ninkinanka*?"

Bass sent her a surprised look. "Don't tell me you've never heard about the legend of the *Ninkinanka*."

Binta's tone turned defensive. "It's not as if I had someone telling me folktales when I was growing up."

Bass put his hand around her shoulders, pulling her closer.

"It is told that, centuries ago, a dragon-like creature called *Ninkinanka* existed within the thickest forests of the country. The creature was so hideous to gaze upon that any ordinary man who sets eyes upon it died instantly out of fear. It was only holy men gifted with spiritual wisdom who could face it and survive."

"And one used to live in this swamp," Junkung put in, picking up a thin stick from the ground and breaking it into tiny bits. "The *Ninkinanka* was the protector of these woods and the community around it. It also used to guard the crowns and other possessions of buried dead kings."

Binta felt a tingle sidle down her spine.

The looming baobab trees seemed to close in around them. It was as if such a creature still existed and lived within the forest.

What was like for the people who lived in ancient times? Did they suffer at the hands of the legendary *Ninkinanka?*

"Don't tell me we've scared you," Bass said against her temple, his fingers tightening around her arm.

"Why would a mere tale about a creature that may or may not have existed scare me?" Binta scoffed.

The two men shared smiles.

"The *Ninkinanka* is just one of several legends," Junkung said. "I'm told that spirits and djinns haunted this woodland and it was considered a very sacred place by the people who lived in the neighbouring villages. They used it to perform tribal rituals such as bathing newly circumcised boys in the waters of the *Manding Bolong*. The kings forbade any hunting and the cutting down of trees in the grounds."

"No wonder the place is so well preserved," Binta commented. "Almost all the trees in our forest reserves have been cut down for industrial use, and the worst part is no efforts are made to replace them. So many wild animals lost their homes as a result."

"Our flora and fauna are almost non-existent now," Bass's tone was rueful.

Junkung stood beside a coconut tree, his expression determined. "That is why we're doing everything in our power to make sure that never happens here. We've made it our personal responsibility to protect this reserve and the animals that live in it."

Binta smiled at him. "You've been doing a pretty good job of it."

Their guide smiled shyly, and they resumed their exploration.

Binta was astounded by the splendid beauty of the birds delicately perched on tree branches. They came in a kaleidoscope of colours, in vibrant greens and reds and oranges. Junkung was pointing them out, telling them their names. There was one he called African paradise flycatcher.

Binta was enthralled by the magnificent small bird. Its feather tale was long and reddish. Its feather breast was black, and so was its sharp little beak. She watched as if flew off, its tiny wings flapping in the sky.

The forest was truly a marvel, a symbol of nature full of its treasures.

A troupe of Western Red Columbus Monkeys walked along a distant clearing. The apes' furs were rich golden hues, their faces dark and distinct.

Lizards scuttled after insects. A cloud of bats hung upside down tree branches.

Binta nudged at Bass to look.

"A mongoose," she muttered in astonishment.

The small animal was elusive as hell. It was almost impossible to find one.

They stared at the lovely cream-furred creature, its head turned in their direction. Its glassy black eyes stared at them for a second before it scampered into the shrubs.

"This forest is amazing," Binta whispered to Bass. "It feels like stepping into a different world altogether."

"Look over there," Bass said, as if he didn't want to spook whatever it was he was looking at.

Binta swivelled.

"Oh," was the only sound that left her mouth.

Bass smiled.

"It's a dwarf deer." He spoke in undertones.

Binta nodded to indicate that she'd heard. Her attention was fixed on the grazing deer.

She couldn't think of any word that could do justice to the animal's loveliness, its grace. Its horns looked like tiny extended branches, its skin a dusky light brown.

There was intelligence in those liquid dark eyes and a sense of security, Binta thought with an indulgent smile.

The animal knew that it was safe within this forest. It was free to wander about as much as it pleased without risking the possibility of being a meal for the predators that were its natural enemies.

Binta wondered about her new-found ability to read the minds of animals as Bass pulled her forward.

She breathed in the scent of blooming flowers, feasted her eyes on their striking petals.

An indescribable joy blossomed in her heart. She would never feel anything like it in any other place. The forest had its own unique charm.

They were in the very middle of the bush, thick with trees that blocked out most of the sunlight.

Junkung maintained a steady flow of conversation, educating them on the various species of plants within sight.

Just before they headed back for the resort, they came upon the most unusual looking tree Binta had ever seen.

"What's this tree called?" she asked Junkung, moving towards it.

"Strangler figs," he replied.

Bass winked at Binta. "Any other name would have been inappropriate."

Binta smiled.

He was right. Its trunk seemed to be made up of many ropes entwined around it. They coiled around the branches in a strangle-like grip and covered the entire ground around the tree, all tangled together.

The trunk felt rough beneath her touch as she ran her fingers through the uneven ridges.

"Amazing," she breathed against the tree.

On their way back to the resort, they spotted a palm wine tapper climbing up a palm tree.

A sling strapped around his waist held him to the tree and supported his balance as his hands and legs crawled upwards.

He job must require a lot of effort and flexibility.

This forest reserve needed preservation for the wildlife habitat and for the people who depended on it for their livelihood.

A few hours after they got back to their lodge, Binta and Bass played a game of cards.

Comfortably seated in the middle of the bed and enjoying the cool air from the hanging ceiling fan, Binta got increasingly annoyed as Bass continued to win round after round.

"Oh, yes!" He threw a fist in the air, claiming victory for the umpteenth time. He grinned from ear to ear. "Who's the unbeatable champion of cards?"

Binta threw her cards on the bed, scowling in irritation. "That's it. I'm out. *Play yah tuma*"

Bass laughed. "Nobody likes a sore loser, Bin."

Before she could find a suitable response to that, she was pushed back on the bed. She couldn't help the giggles that bubbled out of her as Bass lay down beside her and began to nuzzle her neck.

"Do you know what would make our last day here perfect?" he husked against her neck.

"You winning another round of cards?" She sounded out of breath. The butterfly kisses he was raining on her neck were making her head spin.

"That could work too, but I had something else in mind."

She lay on her side, facing him.

Their faces were inches apart, and she couldn't resist the urge to caress his.

"And what's that?"

He climbed out of bed, pulling her along. Binta reluctantly followed him out of the bedroom.

She was a bit exhausted from their tour of the forest although she wasn't complaining. It had been worth it.

There was an African pirogue floating on the river at the edge of their lodge.

"We're going canoeing?"

"Yes, we are," Bass confirmed and helped her step into the wooden dugout canoe.

Binta gingerly sat on the wooden plank inside the canoe with her knees drawn up. Bass sat opposite her, his back to their rower, a teenage boy seated at the far end. He began to row them down the river.

As they drifted down the glistening waters, the mangrove swamp came into view.

There were women collecting oysters from the underwater roots and sunbirds feeding off nectar from the flowers.

The only sounds that could be heard were the continuous plunging of the rower's paddle and the occasional bird calls.

The serenity of the environment was like a soothing balm to her being. She felt relaxed, pressure-free.

Her gaze swung back to Bass and found him staring at her. The deep affection that shone in his eyes overwhelmed her.

The reflections of the setting sun bathed the calm waters in different shades of golden light.

"You've made me so happy, Bass." She could no longer fight the fierce urge to let him know, to somehow communicate what it truly meant to her. "There were times when I believed I would never be, but you've proven me wrong."

"You deserve nothing less, my darling," he murmured softly, the corners of his mouth lifting in a half-smile, "and I will continue to do so if you'll let me."

Who could ever say no to that?

Without giving a second thought to her actions, Binta moved closer to Bass. She greedily inhaled as their lips touched, and they kissed.

Every bone in her body sighed with wondrous joy, her very battered soul filled with bliss.

This was what Bass did to her, take away the darkness caused by years of abuse and replace it with beautiful blinding light.

A light that gave her hope for a better future.

CHAPTER NINE

A week after they returned from their weekend getaway, Binta's bank sent her to Zurich to represent them in an international banking conference. A reward of her hard work and competence.

It was a thoroughly wonderful experience.

Switzerland's capital city was a beauty to behold; ancient colourful architecture mixed with modern-day break-taking skyscrapers.

The conference was a thrilling experience.

She met different kinds of people from all over the world who were passionate about the same things. Finance, Investment, Marketing, and the Stock Market were discussed at length. It was an entire week of business and pleasure, interacting with conference members and touring Zurich.

BETTING ON LOVE

All in all, Binta could say that her life has never been better, both the professional and personal. She stood at the terrace of her hotel, gazing out at a spectacular view, and thinking about Bass. She'd just finished talking to him on the phone.

She didn't know she would miss him this badly. She'd been riding the high of his presence for the past weeks. Now she felt like an addict going through withdrawal.

Bass has become a drug to her, and being deprived of him was the worst form of torture.

However, the week-long conference was almost over.

She would soon be home, in his arms, her absolute favourite place in the world.

THE DAY BINTA GOT BACK to The Gambia, Bass attended a teacher workshop at the Maximus Hotel at Senegambia.

He'd promise to visit her as soon as he was done, but there was no way Binta could wait. After she got home and rested for a few hours, she took a cab and met him at the hotel.

Bass and his colleagues exited the hotel just as the Binta's taxi halted at the entrance. She got out, a huge smile spreading across her face as their gazes met.

Her heart swelled with joy, a joy that mingled with a poignant feeling, a frightening excitement that was inexplicable.

She ran towards him and didn't stop until she was enveloped in his arms.

They both laughed out loud as he lifted her off the ground and not caring who saw, lowered her until they were eye level and kissed her soundly, hungrily.

Binta could tell how much he missed her by the urgency of the kiss, its blatant passion.

"God, I've missed you," he murmured against her mouth in a rough whisper.

"Not as much as I did, you can be sure of that," she replied with a grin and reluctantly pulled out of his arms. "Let's get out of here."

WHEN THEY GOT TO BINTA'S flat, Bass relaxed on the couch and flicked through the channels whilst she made them dinner. She prepared fish and chips and made some *Wonjo* as refreshment.

"That dinner was so delicious," Bass praised as she settled beside him on the couch after they finished eating.

"Was it now?" She shot back smugly right before he cradled her face in his hands.

"It really was," he husked, staring at her slightly open mouth. "I believe you deserve a reward for it."

And the next thing Binta knew Bass had captured her lips in a kiss that melted her heart into a puddle of pleasure.

Her pulse raced at an abnormal pace.

Everything else was blocked out of Binta's mind. She and Bass devoured each other's lips; tasting, exploring, reacquainting. It was every bit as intense and ferocious as their kisses always were and then some.

Binta abruptly pulled back and on a burst of inspiration lay back on the couch.

"Bass, touch me," she invited on a ragged breath.

PANTING HEAVILY, BASS stared at her, lying on the couch, head thrown back. Her face was flushed and eyes closed, ebony skin glistening with desire, lips swollen red from his kisses. She looked so beautiful... so utterly passionate. He had missed her so goddamn much.

How was it possible to want something to the exclusion of everything and everyone else?

How was it possible to need someone so much it seemed as if he didn't have her he would die?

And after the request she has just made, his hands itched to explore her body.

"Open your eyes and look at me, Bin," Bass said.

She complied, and he almost lost the little bit of control he had left.

The swirling depths of passion and lust for him in her eyes did it for him.

With sure hands, he unbuttoned her blouse. His eyes never wavered from hers.

The force of his desire was indescribable, it was palpable, and it felt like electricity running through his veins. It consumed him.

He reached the last button and gently pulled the blouse away. Oh, it felt good to get his hands on all that soft and smooth skin. She gasped as he ran his hand along her abdomen.

"You have the softest skin I have ever touched, do you know that?" he whispered gruffly.

She smiled with slightly trembling lips and then moaned loudly as his hands cupped her bra-covered breasts.

"That feels so good, Bass," she whimpered. "Please, don't stop."

He slipped his hands inside her bra and twisted her nipples, pulling a sharp cry of pleasure from her lips. "I don't plan to. I want to drive you crazy with desire for me."

"You already have," she replied on a sigh. "It's impossible to want you more than I already do."

He caressed her breasts roughly, her moans of pleasure, feeding his lust to a fevered pitch.

His hands trailed down her skirt, and he slipped them under, encountering her honeyed thighs.

He placed one on her pelvis whilst the other slid into her silky panties. His fingers explored her most secret places... all that softness... that wetness scrambled his brain, rendering the ability to think obsolete.

He watched her intently, catching every expression of pleasure on her face, every moan, every cry.

He ever so gently caressed her throbbing feminine nub, and as she bit back a scream, all the blood in his body rushed to one place.

He was so painfully hard that it was a miracle he could function at all.

Her body was tense, ready for release... one more flick of his finger over her clitoris and she lit up like a firecracker at a festival.

He stared at her, barely breathing as a million and one spasms shook her body.

He removed his hands from her body and moved an inch from her on the sofa.

The smile of satisfaction on her face filled his heart with joy. He grinned at her, feeling ridiculously happy despite the painful erection he was nursing in his pants. "Did you enjoy that?"

"Uh-huh," she replied breathlessly, grinning back at him. "I should cook for you more often."

Bass laughed. How he adored this woman. There was no doubt in his mind that he wanted her forever and he couldn't help but think about when the right time will be to let her know this.

CHAPTER TEN

Bass climbed out of the van and stepped into the busy street of Fajara. The non-stop honking of the moving vehicles mingled with the snatches of conversations from passing pedestrians.

The air was heavy with the foul carbon monoxide from the exhaust pumps of cars and motorcycles alike. The sun was slowly descending over the horizon, the brilliance of its light waning.

Bass looked up at the gigantic building that was his father's empire, his family's legacy. Faal Cooperation was a magnificent structure, made entirely of glass, tall and imposing. It made all the other buildings surrounding it pale in comparison.

He walked in, the cool air of the reception area hitting him instantly. The floor was marbled, a flat-

BETTING ON LOVE 159

screen TV was placed in one corner of the wall, showing a CNN news broadcast. Bass greeted the receptionist and proceeded to the private elevator to take him to his elder brother's office.

Abdul Aziz was the vice president of the company and seemed to be doing a damn good job. Their father never failed to sing his praises. He always talked about how relieved he would be when he retired, knowing his company would be in safe hands.

The elevator door pinged open, and Bass walked into the narrow corridor outside. He stepped inside the office of Abdul Aziz's secretary which was adjoined to his own.

Mariama was sitting behind her desk, her fingers typing at her computer's keyboard at the speed of lightning. She looked up as she heard him call out her name and smiled warmly. She was a pretty, young woman with a chocolate complexion and a beautiful hour-glass figure.

Bass knew the reason she had been hired had nothing to do with her feminine endowments, but rather, the fact that she was hard-working and diligent.

"It's good to see you, Basiru," she said, hands folded on her desk. She had on a creamy muslin shirt with several rows of sparkly buttons and a black cotton trouser.

"Likewise, Mariama, how are you? I hope the big boss isn't working you too hard."

She chuckled, crossing her legs. "You know your brother. He's the ultimate slave driver, but he pays me enough not to complain."

Bass shook his head at that.

"Don't let him turn you into the total workaholic without a social life that he is, not for all the money in the world," he said, walking past her. He didn't bother to ask if his brother was busy. He had already informed him that he was coming over.

"I'll keep that in mind," he heard her reply over his shoulder.

Pushing open the door, Bass strode inside, his loafers sinking into the lush soft oriental carpet on the floor. It was a huge office, with golden brocade curtains hanging all around. His brother was not a fan of natural light. He was sitting behind his rectangular mahogany desk, nose buried in a mountain of paperwork.

His head had whipped up at the sound of the door opening. He spared his younger brother a quick glance before returning his attention to the stack of papers that littered his desk.

"Give me a second," he rumbled, sounding distracted.

"Take your time," Bass replied and sat down on one of the twin white leather couches in the room.

Bass leaned into the softness of the seat, his tense shoulders relaxing. He ran his hands over his tired face, sighing in desperation.

He was on a quest that seemed to have little chance of success. He couldn't bear the thought of giving up, not even when despair weighed on his heart.

His gaze landed on his elder brother as he pushed away his documents and rose from his chair. Abdul Aziz was tall, well-built, and classically handsome.

With a complexion that was even fairer than Bass's, women always gave him a second look wherever he went. He was dressed in an expensive well-tailored suit with diamond cufflinks. He wore wealth like a second skin, the epitome of sophistication and charm.

Bass's classmates always teased him, saying that no one would ever know he was from a wealthy family from the way he appeared. His manners were as refined as a street urchin's not to mention he always used to dress like one.

Abdul Aziz, on the other hand, looked, acted, and breathed old money.

He approached with a leisurely gait and sat beside his brother, his dominating presence somehow comforting Bass.

"You look frustrated," his brother observed with a wry grin, placing one leg above the other. "What's going on with you?"

Bass scratched his head, sighing. "How do you always bend people to your will, Abdul? You always get what you want, no matter how impossible the odds are."

Abdul Aziz grinned fully then, his eyes flashing with amusement. "*Dafa* simple really. I study people, learn their weaknesses and exploit them to my advantage."

"*Naka nga fokneh lai muna amae* information from people who, for some reason or the other are reluctant to divulge?" Bass asked his older brother.

"It's the same principle," he replied, resting his chin on his knuckles, his diamond cufflink catching the light of the hanging lamps. "Just figure out what these individuals might want in return and be ready to provide it."

Bass gave this some thought knew precisely what his next move was going to be.

"Does this have anything to do with Binta?" Abdul's perceptive question cut through his thoughts.

He sighed, nodding. "It's a long story, big bro."

Abdul Aziz leaned back against his seat. "I have all the time in the world to listen to it."

"So, it turns out that..."

BY THE TIME BASS LEFT his brother's office, his confidence that the puzzle that was Binta's roots will be solved had significantly increased.

He made one more stop before he went home, dropped in the bank, and withdrew a large sum of money. The night wind was chilly. His street was filled with the haunting notes of the callers for Isha prayers.

He stepped into one of the mosques, and as he supplicated to Allah, he begged for success in his quest.

The next morning, he woke with a single-minded purpose. He was going to find answers about Binta's birth parents.

After dressing in slacks and a shirt, he left for Bundung.

To his surprise, he wasn't unceremoniously thrown out when he announced his relationship with Binta to her adoptive parents. Musu and Babucarr ushered him into their house and offered him a seat.

Bass gingerly settled into one of the scruffy settees, glancing furtively at the decrepit living room. The walls had cracks that ran in straight lines. The wooden stand was broken, eaten away by cockroaches and termites no doubt. It was supporting an old television he was sure was no longer functional.

The older couple sat on the opposite sofa.

Bass tried extremely hard not to be bothered by the squeaking sounds made by what had to be mice in the settee.

As if to confirm his thoughts, two plump ones ran across the room as if they had every right to.

"What brings you by, young man?" Musu asked.

She wore a pale blue *grande boubou,* grey hair peeking from the head-tie. Her expression was wary, just like her husband's.

Babucarr was dressed in a kaftan that must have been white once but was now a dreary grey.

"I want to know the true story of how Binta came into your care," Bass stated.

"My wife already told her when she came here with her friend," Babucarr spoke up, his beady eyes not quiet meeting Bass's. "What more do you want from us? *Amunj dara lunj laa waxh.*"

Outside, the sound of pestle hitting a mortar drifted into the room. "*Gomou mah lolou.* I think you're hiding something and you're going to tell me exactly what that is."

Uncomfortable silence reigned in the room, and it told him that he was unto something.

Bass could now hear the hissing sound of something frying in hot oil. He leaned on his thighs, fixing them with a piercing stare.

"I think you should leave now," Musu said, wringing her hands.

Bass opened his briefcase without replying and withdrew a bulk of cash that amounted to fifty thousand dalasi. He placed it beside him on the settee.

"This money is yours if you want it to be," Bass said. "All you have to do is tell me what I need to know because there is no way people as horrible as you will just take in a helpless child out of the goodness of your hearts, even if it seemed as if you couldn't have children of your own. Given the sorry state of this house, I would say you're sorely in need of cash. If I were you, the right decision would be easy to make."

They exchanged a long look and Bass held his breath, silently praying that this worked. They seemed to have decided not to let an opportunity like this slip through their fingers for Musu started speaking in a quiet tone albeit a clear one.

Bass didn't move a muscle as he listened to the unbelievable tale the old woman spun.

By the end of it, he was outraged, stunned but most unexpectedly hopeful. He was filled with hope for the woman he loved and the future he envisioned they would have together.

CHAPTER ELEVEN

As Binta walked into the Senegambia Villa that is Bass's family home, a rush of nervousness stole over her.

She hadn't set eyes on his family members in ages, and the last time she did, she and Bass were merely friends.

Even though, she'd told Bass she wanted to wait for a while before breaking the news of their relationship to his parents, meeting them still felt like a big deal.

Bass had assured her that the New Year eve's party was an intimate affair, just the family and a few close friends.

The second she appeared on the rooftop of the three-storey building, Bass rushed to her side.

BETTING ON LOVE

He placed a tender kiss on her forehead, and they walked towards his family with their hands linked, the squeeze of his fingers bolstering her courage.

The rooftop was elegantly decorated, a few people she didn't recognize mill about, chatting in small groups.

"*Waw k*i Binta *lah*?" Mustapha Faal, Bass's father, broke into a huge grin and opened his arms.

Binta hesitated for a beat before stepping into his warm embrace.

"Fatoumatta, see how our girl has grown up," he said this with a rumbling laugh, addressing his wife who seemed less enthusiastic to see her.

"Yes, she definitely has," she said, the smile on her beautiful face not quite reaching her eyes.

"Uncle, Aunty, it is good to see you after all these years."

"Likewise, my dear. How have you been?"

"*Ah santa yallah*. I've been good."

"Binta!" Only Sira could shout her name like that.

Next thing, Bass's baby sister barrelled into her arms. Bass just shook his head and laughed.

Binta took in the welcomed sight of Sira who looked lovely in a wine-red catsuit.

"I've missed you so much," she gushed, smiling from ear to ear, her eyes sparkling with exuberance.

"Oh, I've missed you so much more, *janha*," Binta replied with an excited laugh.

"Has Bass told you that I'm married? Come meet my husband!"

And without waiting for an answer, Sira dragged her away.

After Binta was introduced to the husband, she and Sira proceeded to an unoccupied section of the rooftop to catch up.

A while later, Sira had to excuse herself, and Binta was left alone. She leaned against the railing as her gaze sought out Bass's lean figure.

She spotted him on the far end, conversing with Sheriff and Abdul Aziz. She tried to figure out what exactly was the important news he'd promised to relay tonight.

He'd sounded so excited when he called about the party yesterday, saying after the clock struck twelve, he will tell her something that would change everything.

Just then, Bass's mother made towards her accompanied by a woman she'd never seen before.

As they approached, Binta instinctively tensed up.

"Binta, there you are. I thought I would introduce you to Naffie, Bass's fiancé. He doesn't seem particularly inclined to do so."

It was a good thing Binta was leaning against the railing. Otherwise, her legs would have betrayed her, and she would have fallen to the ground.

A buzzing sounded in her head, and the disorienting sensation took over, giving a feeling of detachment from her surroundings.

Like a spectator viewing the scene before her eyes from the side-lines, everything suddenly looked and felt surreal.

She was numb as she shook hands with Naffie and Fatoumatta introduced her as Bass's old friend whom he held in great esteem.

Then the stunning lady walked towards the direction where Bass stood.

"You know, I was thinking, Bin. Perhaps you could talk some sense into Bass. A few months ago, he had a disagreement with Naffie. A lover's tiff. Nothing serious. But that stubborn man is still holding onto his anger. Since you're the only one he listens to, maybe you can convince him to let it go."

Binta nodded with a strained smile for lack of a better thing to do. She watched, her heart shrivelling in her chest with every second that passed as Naffie grabbed Bass's hand and pulled him away from his brother and friend. He yanked his hand out in the same breath, said something to her angrily and then walked past her, his gaze searching.

Binta knew that he was looking for her. She turned on her heels and ran, but it was already too late because he was shouting her name and begging her to stop.

She didn't. Not until she reached the front yard garden and that was only because she realised she couldn't just leave without venting out what was in her heart.

When she whirled around, he was almost upon her, their breathing laboured from the running.

For a second, she just stared at his face, hating the fact that because of him, her heart which was no stranger to pain was filled with it.

But this misery gripping her soul was a clear manifestation that she was yet to know real torment.

If she continued with this relationship and fell deeper for this man, she would risk it all.

That's when she knew that even if his mother hadn't been truthful, she had to pull the plug, had to retreat into safety or there would come a day when her feelings would break her into pieces.

"Is she really your fiancé, Bass?"

"What? Of course not." His reply was quick in coming. "I mean, she was. I broke off the engagement a few months ago."

Binta believed him. She had no reason not to, Bass has never lied to her.

But instead of easing away, her desire to run was intensifying.

"She and your mother have a different opinion on the matter. Were you going to tell me you had a fiancé?" She threw the question in his face.

"I would have told you eventually. If it was really that important to our relationship, I would have said something earlier."

"Your mom did this because she suspects there is something between us, and it's not something she wants. And given the fact that I've had enough rejection to last me a lifetime, I have no plans of encountering more, especially from your mother."

"Bin, my mom is just mad that I broke up with Naffie. She's her pet. But of course, she would be on board once we make known our relationship. She's always liked you." He said in a soft voice and tried to pull her into his arms.

To him, the matter was settled.

She took a step back.

"Yes, as your friend she has, but your mother wants to see you with a girl like Naffie, and like I said, I won't deal with any more rejection."

"What exactly are you trying to say here, Bin?" He asked the question slowly, his expression grim.

It was as if he already knew where this was going. As if there was a part of him that knew this day would come.

Binta couldn't stand to look at him as the next words she uttered slip out of her mouth. "I think we've had a good run and we should call it quits before things start getting messy and... and..."

"And what, Bin?"

"We could cause each other a great deal of suffering, Bass."

"That's the risk that comes with love. I thought you understood that by now and accepted it."

"That's what I thought too but what happened today made me realise I'm not capable of putting my faith in something I can't control and I did not build myself up only to be destroyed by love."

"Then walk away. Walk out of this compound and know for sure that you've broken my heart for the last time. If we've come this far and you still can't believe, still can't bet on the love we've felt for each other for all these years, then you never will and frankly, I don't want to build my life with someone who only sees love as a threat that would bring her world crashing down."

Binta found it impossible to swallow the lump in her throat.

She wanted to rush into his arms, to kiss him with the passion she carried in her heart. To tell him that, yes, he was right when he said they've loved each other for the past five years and that she was sure they were going to for the rest of their lives.

Then Musu's malicious face flashed in her mind.

So instead, she turned around and ran.

CHAPTER TWELVE

"*Chaapan*," Binta cursed out savagely as her finger got stuck on the door of the refrigerator.

She jumped around a bit as the pain spread through her hand and intensified. So did her cursing.

She would have easily prevented the incident if she wasn't going around the apartment stumping and banging everything in her wake.

The anger and hurt burning her from the inside out simply needed some sort of release.

She didn't understand this widening void created in her heart since the fateful night she ran away from Bass.

She had expected pain, yes, and a sense of loss over the breakup but not this gripping emptiness threatening her sanity.

She couldn't do away with it, not even knowing where to start.

What was maddening was the tendril of regret crawling around her heart.

Part of her wanted to turn back time and do things differently, to be bolder, to take that leap of faith Bass had been desperately asking for.

She slumped on the tiled floor and leaned back against the refrigerator.

More than anything else, she wanted to know how he was doing. The idea of his suffering cut her deeper than she cared to examine.

Mai had called earlier, offering to take her out since it was a Sunday or at least keep her company and she'd turned down both offers. She didn't want to go out or see anyone, not even her best friend.

Her hand closed tightly around her phone as her mind raced with conflicting thoughts.

She could call Bass, couldn't she? Surely, there was nothing wrong with wanting to hear his voice and ask how he was doing?

And before she could stop herself, she swiped the phone open and dialled his number.

Her thumping heartbeat reverberated in her head in tandem with the ringing on the other line.

"Hello, Bin," His voice sounded distant, polite but withdrawn.

She felt a rising panic. She had to put the phone away for a second to stifle a sob.

"Bass... um... hi... I wanted to know how you are doing."

She must sound stupid. Calling someone to enquire about someone's wellbeing after breaking their heart was nothing if not sadistic.

"I'm not doing great, but I'm not running around screaming at the top of my lungs either," he said this in a voice that had softened. "Look, don't drown yourself in guilt. I knew getting involved with you could go either way, yet I still chose to put my heart on the line again, and I don't regret it. Just take care of yourself, okay. Don't worry about me."

Her lower lip trembled, and she nodded as if he could see her.

"Bass... I... I think..." It was on the tip of her tongue to tell him that she made a mistake and to beg him to take her back. She trailed off instead. The words just wouldn't come out.

"Yes?" he prompted.

"Never mind. I will do as you say. I will try to do away with the guilt now that I know you will be fine. Do find it in your heart to forgive me."

"Like I said, I knew what I was getting into. Goodbye, Bin."

And with that, he ended the call.

Her head hit the tiled floor as the loud sobs racked her body. She let out a blood-curdling scream and placed her hand over her heart. It felt as if she was dying on the inside.

The sound of knocking on her front door penetrated her world of torment.

She rose from the floor, hurriedly rinsed her face in the sink and rushed to open the door, wishing that it was Mai even though she'd told her not to come.

When she pushed open the door, she found a middle-aged woman she had never set eyes on standing on the other end.

The woman was well-dressed and strikingly beautiful. There was an air of affluence about her that was unmistakable. She looked nervous, which further puzzled Binta.

"Are you Binta Ceesay?" she asked, her fingers fidgeting over the handle of her designer handbag.

"Yes, I am. Please come in," Binta said with a smile to put the mysterious stranger at ease.

She returned the smile and followed Binta inside.

"Can I get you something?" she asked as the woman sat down on the couch.

"A glass of water would be nice."

Binta nodded and walked into the kitchen. She noticed that her hands were trembling as she poured the cool liquid into a glass.

Although her expression hadn't let it on, there was something about this woman that put her off balance.

Where did she come from, and what did she want?

The questions race in her head as she walked back into the sitting room. She handed over the glass and sat down beside her.

The woman drank the water in one gulp and turned to stare at Binta. Her gaze was unflinching, and the expression in their depths was a wild one.

It was as if she was in awe as if she couldn't believe who her eyes were taking in.

Binta's heart thumped hard as a dangerous idea slithered its way into her head.

"Who are you if you don't mind me asking?"

The woman diverted her gaze for a second, and this time tears welled into her eyes when she met Binta's gaze. "My name is Mariama Cham... and I believe I'm your mother."

"My mother?" Binta croaked out.

A cold numbness was fast gripping her, and she instinctively knew that wherever this woman had been, Bass found her.

"What makes you think you are my mother?"

"Well, a few weeks back, a young man called Basiru Faal came to me. He told me that I was the biological mother of his girlfriend. Her adoptive parents confided in him they had been paid to raise her."

"Paid to raise? Bass told you this?" None of this made sense. Binta's head was heavy, filled with a distracting, buzzing sound.

"I understand your confusion but let me narrate this story from the beginning. I got pregnant at seventeen. My father, a well-known and respected man from the wealthy Joben family of Serrekunda, was furious. I had brought humiliation upon the family. I was hidden during the period of the pregnancy. Your father had abandoned me. It was a difficult birth. I had to be operated upon. When I came to, I was told that I had given birth to a stillborn. A dead baby was presented to me. I remember crying so much that the blanket the baby was wrapped in became soaked," she paused after saying this.

Her eyes welling up with tears as she stared at her daughter. Binta got the impression she was reliving that moment she'd held her supposed dead baby in her arms.

"A few weeks later," she said, "my parents shipped me off to America. They said it was the best place for university studies, but I could tell they desperately wanted me out of the country. My husband and I decided to come back to The Gambia with our two sons recently. When Basiru came to me and told me about how my parents had paid Musu and Babucarr to raise you, I didn't want to believe it. For two reasons. I was afraid to open myself to the possibility that I had a daughter out there. I did not want to believe that my parents had gone that far to separate me from my baby. But when I confronted them about it, they came clean. Told me I had been too young to be a mother. My future would have been ruined. Basiru told me where to find you."

Binta bounded off the couch before the woman even finished her last sentence. Turning her back to the woman, she stood so very still, her hands fisted by her sides.

She didn't know what to think, how to feel. Her life suddenly resembled a beautiful fantasy where her biggest dream was in the process of being fulfilled, her greatest fear taken away.

She had been wanted.

Dear Lord, she had been loved by the woman who'd brought her into this world.

She jerked out of the trance she didn't realise she'd fallen into when she felt a hand on her shoulder. She swivelled around and threw herself into the arms of her mother.

Binta couldn't tell who was sobbing louder as they clung to each other. They were tears of regret of time lost and tears of joy of the time yet to come.

After the crying stopped, they huddled together on the couch and talked for hours.

Mariama talked about how she'd mourned the daughter she believed she'd lost and how throughout the years, she'd always wondered what she would have been like had she lived.

To her, finding Binta was a miracle, something she was still grappling to wrap her head around.

Binta told her she felt the same. She had given up hope that she would ever find her real parents. And in a way she'd been relieved because she really had been afraid to discover the reason why she was given away.

WHEN MARIAMA REQUESTED that Binta spend a few weeks at her house in Brusubi, she accepted without hesitation.

Living in that house felt to her like being transported into an entirely different planet. The love and care that was showered upon her by her mother and brothers was overwhelming.

BETTING ON LOVE

Even Musa, her mother's husband treated her like a daughter, and it wasn't long before she let down her guard and returned the affection they so readily gave.

She understood this was what a family should be like, living in a home where she was genuinely wanted.

She was in a cocoon of warmth and safety, and all the doubts she harboured about being unlovable slipped away with each passing day.

Thoughts of Bass plagued her, making her regret what she threw away.

She confided this to her mother one evening as they sat in the high-backed chairs in the veranda.

"He's done nothing but love me, *Yaa,* and I have done nothing but hurt him and push him away in return. If it weren't for him, you and I wouldn't have even found each other. And it didn't take me a minute to destroy what we had."

"Do you want him back?"

"With all my heart but I can't help thinking I don't deserve him and he's better off with someone else."

"What nonsense!" her mother admonished with a shake of her head. "You are the one he wants, so nobody's better for him. You've made mistakes, that's for sure, but considering everything you've gone through, they were inevitable. Now that you've realised how much he means to you, this is not the time to sit around and mope. I've meant to tell you how proud I am of the woman you've become. I know your life has been a constant battle and everything you have now you've had to fight for. Now in the same vein, you must fight for your love. Don't let Basiru go. One look at that young man and I could tell how much he loved you. And for your information, I won't accept anybody else as a son-in-law."

"*Yaa*!" Binta said, half laughing, half crying. "You are right, though. It's my turn to fight for this love. Do you think he will take me back?"

"My dear, he wouldn't know how to say no even if he wants to. How do you feel about huge romantic gestures?"

"They are always my favourite part of romance movies."

"Then it's time you get to work."

THE ANNUAL SPEECH AND award ceremony held at Nusrat Senior Secondary School was in full swing when Bass and Sheriff arrived. The school hall was packed to overflowing.

Sheriff sat down on one of the few available chairs in the last row while Bass squeezed his way to the first row where his seat was reserved with the other teachers.

It was not his intention to come late to one of his favourite school events of the year, but Sheriff had had an emergency that caused their delay.

Bass loved seeing deserving students and teachers got rewarded for their excellence and hard work.

The pride that always lit up an awardee's family members' faces was still a joy to behold.

A fog of melancholy floated around his heart as his thoughts flitted to Binta.

Her mother had called him earlier in the week, thanking him profusely for uniting them. She had then asked about his schedule for the next few days, whether there was anything he was looking forward to attending.

He had found the questions odd but had told her about the award ceremony anyways.

He was happy that Binta finally had the family she deserved. He was comforted knowing she wasn't alone and surely she must believe by now that she deserved only good things.

He mentally shook himself.

No need spending time thinking of his lost love. It wouldn't change anything.

He turned his focus on what was going on around him—no more dwelling on the past.

There was a funny but educative play being performed on the stage by the school's drama group. He laughed like everybody else at the students' portrayal of cheating attempts during exams.

After the play ended and the actors left the stage accompanied by thunderous clapping. They started giving out prizes for best teacher by subject. Bass stood up and applauded as a close friend was awarded best Chemistry teacher. He hugged him and teased him about them sharing the prize when he returned from the stage.

Bass whipped his head from his phone as his name was announced as the best Mathematics teacher.

He got up gingerly, his ears ringing, his heart thumping with joy and excitement as he made his way to the stage.

"Ladies and gentlemen," The MC, Mr Bayo, an English and Literature teacher, said into the microphone with a conspiratorial smile as he stared at Bass. "Although this is not the norm, Mr Faal's award is going to be presented to him by a lady who claims he means the world to her. You can come out now."

Binta emerged on the stage.

Bass forgot how to breathe as he stared at her, frozen to the spot where he stood.

Mr Bayo handed her the microphone and the prize. She looked like an ebony goddess in the shimmering sky-blue ankle-length Ankara gown she wore.

Her eyes communicated her nervousness, but Bass could also swear he had never seen so much love and determination reflected in their depths.

He wanted to run to her in that instant and tell her she was forgiven even before she could say a word, but he resisted the urge.

Today he wanted to feel chosen by this woman. As he had always given himself to her without a single thought, today he wanted to be wooed.

He didn't want to make it look like it was okay for her to walk away anytime she felt like it.

So, he remained standing and stared at her with a neutral expression on his face.

The hall had gotten as silent as a graveyard. Everybody's attention was on Binta. It was as if like Bass, they were all holding their breaths, waiting for what she would do next.

She raised the microphone to her lips and began to speak in a voice that trembled.

"This is where it all started. In this school. Our friendship. Our love. Because of you, I knew there was more to life than pain and loneliness. You taught me how to laugh and hope even in the face of great difficulty."

Her throat bobbed as she swallowed.

"And I have loved you for it in a way I didn't know I was capable of. You became an extension of me, a mirror in which I see the best version of myself. Which—"

She sucked in a breath, her body shuddering before she continued, eyes glued to him.

"Which is why I've been so afraid to completely give in to the love we've always shared. I never thought I had enough strength to put myself back together if we were to break apart. I was wrong. So very wrong. I see that now. Love, just like life has no guarantee. It's beyond our control, but that doesn't mean we shouldn't try. So here I am asking you to take a chance on me. I've realised that playing it safe is no way to live. I'm ready to throw caution to the wind and bet on our love. If you will still have," she finished on a breathless note.

"By the way, you will have to take me back if you want your prize."

Now the silence was no more. The hall was filled with applause and jeering and intelligible murmurs.

Bass drowned out all the noise. His attention was solely on the woman who'd just laid her heart bare.

"Bin," Bass said her name in a low soft tone.

"Yes," she whispered back. The look of expectant hope in her eyes was almost his undoing.

"Will you please hand over my prize?"

And just like that she dropped the microphone and the prize and rushed into his arms.

He held her tight, so tight there was no air left to breathe.

As the deafening roar of applause resounded in the hall, Bass whispered in the ear of the woman he loved,

"Make sure you pack this dress first for our honeymoon."

Thank you for reading Betting on Love.

If you enjoyed this story, please leave a review on the site of purchase.

ABOU THE AUTHOR

Kani Sey is the penname of a young Gambian woman living and studying in Morocco. She's always loved reading and began writing at an early age. She's passionate about books, movies, and music. Her one true dream is to become a successful, prolific writer.

Connect with Kani:

Facebook: https://facebook.com/adam.nyang.7

Instagram: https://www.instagram.com/adam_chumbay/

GLOSSARY

Wolof – English

Gaenal fi: Get out
Suma yoon nekusi: It's none of my business
Yaa, nyan nala: Mum, please
Yaa: Mum
ningaa nyaka jom: Shameless girl
falleh wulen: you don't care
Bul worry: Don't worry
Nexh rek lenj def: They are so delicious
time bu barri lah: Is a very long time
Dama over surprise sah: I was really surprised
Yaa gena hamneh: You know very well
Chopsa binga done: You are such a foodie
Hamnga: You know
Baxhna: Alright

Suma: My

Understand *naa:* I understand

Bai ma dem hol: Let me go see

Lee purr yow lah: This is for you

Jere jeff y: Thanks a lot

Bai mah: Let me

Lan lah: What is it?

Mashalla, jangha sanjseh ngah: Dear God, woman, you look beautiful

Bayil tonj: Stop with the flattery

Halehbi dafa over daegerr bopah: The girl is really stubborn

Lolou degalah: That is true

Yowtamit: C'mon

Giss ngah asahman bi num mel: You see how dark the sky is

Bull mah waxh neh: Don't tell me

Ndo bi: The woman

Hamnaa neh: I know

Halatuma won sah: I didn't even think about

Nyu dem si biir: Let's go

Lutaxh: Why
Suma hamon neh|: If I had known
Daeded: No
Foguma: I don't think
Halatuma koh sah: I'm not even thinking about it
Yowtamit: C'mon
Baxhna, baxhna: Alright, alright
Lolou nga buga mah def: Is that what you want me to do?
Daeded: No
Kon: Then
Play yah tuma: I won't play anymore
Dafa: It's
Naka nga fokneh lai muna amae: What is the best way to get
Amunj dara lunj laa waxh: We have nothing else to say to you
Gomou mah lolou: I don't believe that
*Waw k*i Binta *lah:* Is this really Binta?
Ah santa yallah: Ah thank God

Janha: It literally means young woman but is often used as a term of endearment

Chaapan: It's a curse word. There is no English equivalent

Yaa: Mom

Keep reading for chapter one from *Beautiful Mess* by Mukami Ngari.

BLURB

Makena and Daniel meet at the beach and a whirlwind romance begins. But the past comes calling when she finds out that her father murdered Daniel's dad. The only man she loves is the one she can never be with. Is their love strong enough to overcome the dark past?

BEAUTIFUL MESS - CHAPTER ONE

~~Makena~~

August 2012

Even to this day, I enjoy travelling. I find little pieces of God when I'm inside a moving car, looking out the window, watching the people and the trees move backwards. There is something about these moments that just factory resets my mind.

The soft sound of snoring occasionally distracts me. My best friends, Wanja and Nduta, have been asleep for six out of seven hours of the journey, while I've stayed awake.

The bus pulls to a stop. We are here, in Mombasa.

Finally, warm air hits my nostrils as we get off the bus. The turquoise waters of the Indian Ocean sparkle in my peripheral vision. Going down to the beach is on my bucket list.

There is that thing I must do, for my sanity's sake and for my dear mother.

I feel for the yellow thing in my bag, buried under my blue Sunday best dress and my beaded sandals.

Mombasa is hotter than any place I've been, but I'm too excited to complain. Instead, I take off my brown knit sweater and stuff it in my bag. I wiggle my sweaty toes, inside my black plastic shoes.

"Tosh." Nduta drops her bag and starts running.

Turning around, I see her boyfriend. His name is Gitonga, but we call him Tosh. His family owns the one and only posho mill in the village.

Tosh and Nduta hug and kiss and laugh. They haven't seen each other in three months.

Looking at them makes me wonder how it feels, how love feels. I've never found a boy who excites me enough.

Tosh sees Wanja and me standing by the corner. We wave, and he frowns.

"Sorry...until you pay her dowry, expect this lot," I tell him as we hug.

His perfume is a little too strong for me. I crinkle my nose.

"It's okay. She is worth it." He smiles.

Nduta blushes and stares at her feet.

Wanja and I approve of him. He is sweet and kind to our girl.

"Loyal too," Wanja would add whenever we speak of Tosh. She is on Facebook as Alicious de Pretty.

And all the pictures on Tosh's social media pages are of Nduta.

Wanja asked one of her pretty college friends to try him and see if he would fall. The friend messaged Tosh some pictures, but he never replied.

He is a cool guy without many words. Although, I don't like how he texts Nduta with stupid spelling mistakes—sweetat, my daling, plecious.

"English is not our tongue...it came on a boat," Nduta always defends her sweetheart.

Tosh looks different from when I last saw him. He's added some weight around the midsection, which is a sign of wealth back home. The job at the port must be paying well. He's grown a beard and a moustache too. He looks all serious and grown-up.

"It's good to see you, Tosh." Wanja squeezes him into a hug.

"Ehen, let's go, my beautiful girls. And stick close to me before someone steals you." Tosh laughs at his own joke.

He walks in front, holding Nduta's hand. Wanja and I follow closely behind, on the path he is parting through the busy streets.

There are ancient houses, Arabic-design mosques, tuk-tuks, and women wearing diras walking with the men in kaptulas, exchanging Mashallahs between them.

Ah, this place is perfect.

In my Heaven, there will be a little section that looks like Mombasa.

We arrive at Tosh's place sooner than I want. His house is in a row of cream-coloured houses with the paints peeling off. The cream and black patches remind me of burnt chapati. His door is marked '7' in black.

"Welcome." Tosh opens the door.

The home is unlike any I've been in. Everything is in one room—the metal-frame bed, kitchen, small TV, low table—and a door leads to the toilet, which doubles as the bathroom.

The place is tidy and smells of his strong perfume. He presses a button on a remote, and soothing RnB music breezes through the room.

"Is that Burning Passion?" Nduta asks about the Mexican soap opera playing on the TV. It is her favourite show.

"Yes." Tosh smiles.

Paloma and Diego, the Romeo and Juliet of the show kiss on-screen. They are hiding behind her father's barn, their rendezvous point.

Wanja and I sit on two plastic stools. Tosh and Nduta are on the bed, exchanging smiles.

I feel a little pang of envy.

"You girls must be hungry." Tosh stands, ready to buy food and reaches for a green paper bag under the glass coffee table, the prettiest thing in the house.

"Tosh, why are you insulting me like this?" Nduta hangs her head. She tries to look cute and disappointed at the same time.

She attended Iregi Catering School and caters at the weddings and funerals back home.

She's one of the best cooks I know. She has a gift. No matter how many times she teaches me how to cook pilau, the amount of garlic needed, or how much Royco cubes to put in beef stew, my food never tastes as good as hers.

"I will cook," she says and reaches for her bag at the foot of the bed. She pulls out a leso, ties it around her waist and heads to the kitchen area.

Tosh smiles, her 'wife material' points probably increasing in his head.

An hour later, we indulge in extremely sweet biryani. Tosh feeds Nduta.

I watch them and pray for a boy like Tosh but without a potbelly and better-smelling cologne.

A knock sounds at the door. Wanja opens since she is closest to it.

"Oooh, babe," she shouts and flings her arms around the tall, brown-skinned Somali guy with soft curly hair. He's in a red Manchester United shirt. Then she kisses him full on the mouth.

My cheeks heat up. I count all my toes close to four times before they come up for air.

Wanja introduces the guy as Noor, her boyfriend from college. Nduta and I look at each other. So, this is the legendary Noor?

Wanja talks about him all the time. They slept together eleven times. She tells us everything while we're on the way to the market, hurdling and whispering like we always do

He's very handsome with big bright eyes and hot pink lips. He sits, and Wanja climbs astride him. They kiss and grope each other as if their world is dark.

"I missed you, babe."

Noor unzips Wanja's blue jeans pants and slips his hand inside there. Wanja purrs like a cat in heat.

I stare at my bag, wishing to fit in it.

He whispers something to her, and they stand. He takes her tiny purple suitcase from the floor, and they wear their shoes.

"See you tomorrow, my kinsmen," Wanja blows kisses in the air as they run out of the place.

AFTER WANJA LEAVES, it's just Tosh, Nduta and me, the third wheel.

As the only one without a boyfriend, I shouldn't have come. I squirm uncomfortably.

"How is everyone back at home?" Tosh asks.

I tell him about the long rains, the newly-weds, the fresh headteacher at the primary school, the recently built church by the river and the story everyone is talking about.

"You remember Wa Muthoni? The woman who sold peanuts along Ena Road. She was crossing the road to grab a customer when a vehicle appeared out of nowhere and 'phu' she was squashed like a watery cabbage."

"Eeyy!" Tosh exclaims.

"It was a 'very very shiny' black Mercedes, but the driver hasn't been caught because all the witnesses are the idlers at the bus station. People are saying the Mercedes man paid them for their silence. But God is not a human being. One of them, Gicara, you remember him? The one who walks with a limp, yes, that one, a muvariti tree fell on him the other day, and he died."

"Very sad," Tosh says. "I feel for her little children. They are four, right? The last one is what? Two years old?"

"He is one, and a half…It's just sad," Nduta replies and Tosh caresses her back in consolation.

"How about you…how have you been?" I ask.

"Like is okay. I can't complain." Tosh rubs his stomach. "But I'm lonely, you know. I miss my sweetheart. Life is extremely hard without her."

He looks at Nduta and caresses her chin slowly, as his throat ripples.

"I will...let me go out and get some air," I excuse myself and step out on the veranda.

Tosh raises the volume of his radio.

I take a walk around the block. The air smells of masala, ginger, and garlic. Mothers are preparing supper and calling their children back home.

A group of little boys are playing football on a dusty field near a filthy dumpsite. One of the boys tells his little brother to go back to the house, but the little brother doesn't listen and keeps following him. They never pass the ball to the youngest boy, but he keeps running after it and tripping each time.

I return to the house an hour later.

Nduta is in the kitchen area, washing utensils and preparing supper. Tosh is on the bed snoring. He sounds like a power saw running out of fuel.

That night Tosh gives me a mattress to place on the floor, moving the coffee table aside. He creeps into bed next to Nduta. It's a little room, and I hear all the grunts and moans they make half of the night. I almost crawl out and sleep on the veranda instead, and when it becomes too much, I think about cutting out my ears.

When I get the chance, I will strangle both my friends. This isn't why I lied to my sweet mother.

The lie: We are attending a church revival in Nairobi.

The plan: We visit Mombasa and tour the coastal town. My friends will say hi to their boyfriends for like an hour or two. Then we all head to a club, dance the night away and get drunk in this city where no one knows us—it will be my first time getting drunk, and I've been looking forward to it. I shouldn't be the only twenty-one-year-old yet to do it.

Afterwards, we'll take the evening bus, return to our little town, and tell our parents that the church revival was such a blessing. Mother will be so proud. She always wants me to take my relationship with Jesus to the next level.

THE NEXT MORNING AT dawn, I tell Nduta and Tosh that I will tour Mombasa independently. They need time alone, and I don't want to keep being the third wheel. Wanja hasn't come back. She's still at Noor's place. The return ticket is for the 10 pm bus, so I have a whole day to explore.

"I'll meet you at the bus stop at 9:30," I tell Nduta. "Tell Wanja the same when she asks."

"*Sawa*," Nduta says.

My mission: go straight to the beach, watch the beautiful blue waters and finally, get rid of the yellow thing in my bag.

However, I make so many stops along the way. First, I buy a coconut and drink from it. It's not as sweet as I thought it would be, so I throw it away.

I think of going to Marikiti market. Instead, I visit Fort Jesus, the fortress where the Portuguese fought the British for the coastal strip.

I want to retrace my steps to Marikiti market. What for? He can't be around there still, can he? What if this is my only chance to see him? Think Makena think.

I go back.

Five months ago, our pastor, Dr Dr Humphrey—yes, he uses the title twice—had a vision about me. I told him in secret once about how I yearn to meet my father, and he told me he would pray for me.

Three days later, he comes out of his fast and calls me to his office. He tells me he knows my father's location—God showed him in a dream.

At the prospect of a reunion, my heart plays a crazy fast soundtrack that makes my knees weak. I take a sit to listen to the good news.

"I saw him, Makena…I saw him in a dream. He looks just like you," he says.

I believe because mother once confirmed it, that one time when I was seven. I fought with a boy in my class, Mutemi, who liked putting frogs in my school bag. He also called me bush hair because I had a very thick mane. One day, fed up with his 'bush hair' taunts, I beat him up until he peed on himself.

Aggrieved, Mother comes to the principal's office, and I know the moment we get home, she'll give me the beating of a lifetime. Mother never spares the rod.

She surprises me, not punishing me as I expect, but not speaking to me either. This is too much a punishment for me to bear. I wish for her to flog me instead.

In the evening, after supper, as we warm ourselves by the fire, she speaks.

"You look like him, you know. Your eyes, your hair ... your skin. You look just like your father, but you will not turn out like him. Do you hear me, Makena?"

"Y—yes," I stutter, ready to promise anything in exchange for her forgiveness.

"You will not turn out like him, and you will not fight again at school, or anywhere." She spits in the fire, and the firewood hisses.

I don't sleep that night, thinking about my father who I look like.

So, when Pastor Humphrey goes on, "He was coming out of a big gold shiny car...and he wore a beautiful black suit, and his shoes were polished...he wore gold rings on all his fingers I tell you."

His words stun me. I put my hands on my mouth. My father is a rich man?

"He walked into a market. At first, I did not know which market it was, but God whispered that it was Marikiti in Mombasa. Everywhere he walked, people bowed down for him. He bought all the things in the market. You should have seen how the traders praised him, Makena. They hugged his knees and thanked him as they closed their stalls early."

"He...bought all the things?" I try to stitch the fragments of this puzzle together.

Maybe my father owns a large hotel. My God, what if he has one or two of those five-star tourist hotels advertised in the paper? My luck in life is about to change.

Mami's arthritis has grown worse. I spend all my salary buying her medication. If my father is a rich man, maybe, he can help us.

"I can take you to see him, Makena" Pastor Humphrey says.

I'm so overwhelmed by his kindness that tears fill my eyes.

"If you want we can go to Mombasa next weekend...just me and you" He winks at me and fondles my hand.

I quickly snatch myself from his married hands.

"It's alright, pastor. I do not want to take you from God's work. I will look for him myself."

I walk out of his office with a headache.

People say he has the gift of prophecy, so the vision must be real. I only wished he had not winked at me.

Now I'm in Mombasa. I can find my father myself. I enter the market and approach the third stall, which has big healthy-looking juicy mangoes.

My father may have bought mangoes here for his big hotel. I stop in front of the trader who sits next to his goods. He is staring at his feet.

"*Samahani...habari yako?*" I call out.

He doesn't seem to hear me.

"*Habari yako?*" I edge closer.

He doesn't hear me or pretends not to.

I nod and walk on. This is crazy, and a sign that I should abandon this mission altogether. It's getting too hot, and I don't have all day. I should go to the beach and do what I'm here to do. I decide to ask one more trader and then leave.

I stop at a tomato stall. There are all kinds of tomatoes, big, and small, some red and ripe and others green. The trader is separating them into three lots. She is a middle-aged woman with a red leso tied around her non-existent waist.

The leso reads, "*Mbuzi kala mkeka, wadaku mtakaa?* The goat has eaten the mat, where will you gossipers sit?"

"*Samahani.* Sorry for bothering you."

"Ehen."

"*Natafta mtu.* I am looking for someone."

Shy suddenly, I wonder how my rusty Swahili sounds to her. Although I'm fluent, I'm not a native.

She goes on separating her tomatoes, and I take that as an encouragement to continue.

"I am looking for the man ... who ... bought all the goods in the market."

She stops and looks at me, up and down. See, she must have met him, and now realises I look exactly like him.

It's happening. Pastor Humphrey may have weak flesh, but his spirit is strong.

"*Ati kafanya nini?*"

"He bought all the goods in the market from all the traders."

She looks into my eyes for a long time. Then drops the tomato she is holding back to the bunch. She tells me not to move and goes to the next stall, where three women sit. They have coconuts, mirrors, lipsticks, and bananas in the disorganised booth. She returns with the women.

"*Rudia ulichosema*. Could you repeat what you just said, please?"

"I am looking for the man who bought all the goods in the market. He wears gold rings on all his fingers."

First, they stare at me, then at each other. Suddenly they burst into loud laughter, holding their shapeless sides. Everyone in the market turns and watches us.

"*Wacha bangi*. Stop smoking whatever you are smoking."

"These youngsters in Mombasa are smoking anything and everything."

The tomato trader holds me by the shoulders. "*Wewe Mrembo*. You are a beautiful girl. Stop smoking these things, eeh. They will destroy your mind. If you have no job, why not go to Diani. You might catch yourself a rich white man."

I shrug and march away fast, keeping my eyes down because everyone is looking at me. Stupid stupid me. Why did I ruin a beautiful trip by coming here?

One of the women, the one with the black henna on her nails and palms runs towards me.

"Dada, sister, maybe I can help. You said he did what again?"

I look into her kajal-rimmed eyes. Maybe someone did know my father after all.

"He bought all the goods—"

Before I finish, she is howling on the ground, and her friends high-five each other as they continue laughing at me.

Funny, how it's no longer funny when the joke is you. I hurry, not looking back.

Don't cry, no crying. I unzip my bag and withdraw my earphones. I put them on although I'm not listening to any music.

BETTING ON LOVE

I flag down a tuk-tuk and head to the beach. Soon I'm there.

Forget those women and do what you came to do, Makena.

I reach for the yellow thing in my bag, and a big lump clogs my pipes. Glancing around, no one is watching. It's time to part ways.

A tear falls from my eyes. Not only for what I'm about to do, but for the incident at the market, and a father I'll never meet. This is harder than I thought.

I grab the yellow thing and yank it out of my bag.

Someone groans behind me, he sounds like he is dying.

I glance over my shoulder.

OTHER BOOKS BY LOVE AFRICA PRESS

Love Happens Eventually by Feyi Aina
Fine Scotch by Emem Bassey
Scars, Secrets & Scores: The Ben & Selina Trilogy by Kiru Taye
Beautiful Mess by Mukami Ngari
Ties That Bind by Stanley Umezulike

CONNECT WITH US

Facebook.com/LoveAfricaPress
Twitter.com/LoveAfricaPress
Instagram.com/LoveAfricaPress
Sign up for news about our upcoming book releases:
www.loveafricapress.com[1]/newsletter

---

1. http://www.loveafricapress.com

BETTING ON LOVE

Milton Keynes UK
Ingram Content Group UK Ltd.
UKHW041218021124
450589UK00005B/451

9 781914 226632